# Mail Order Abigail

Book One of
Sweet Willow Mail Order Brides

Charlotte Dearing

The right of Charlotte Dearing to be identified as author of this Work has been asserted by her in accordance with sections 77 and 78 of the Copyright, Designs and Patents Act of 1988.

Copyright © 2020, 2023 by Charlotte Dearing.
All rights reserved.

No part of this book may be reproduced in any form or by any electronic or mechanical means, including information storage and retrieval systems, without written permission from the author, except for the use of brief quotations in a book review.

This is a clean, wholesome love story set in late 19th century Texas. The hero is strong, successful, and worried. He suddenly has a baby to raise, his nephew, and no idea how to do it. He sends for a mail order bride, and thinks he knows what to expect... an older, sensible Boston woman from a good family... but, like his neighbor had warned, *that ain't what's stepping off the boat.*

# Chapter One

**Abigail Winthrop**

Abigail Winthrop had never been aboard a ship, and after this experience, wasn't sure she'd ever want to be on another. She and her employer, Miss Peabody, stood in silence while their eyes adjusted to the shadows of the steerage quarters, the smell of farm animals and muck heavy in the air.

Slowly her eyes took in the sight, and what she saw disgusted her. Straw, mud and manure were strewn across the floor of the second-class cabins, a far cry from the polished mahogany and velvet curtains upstairs.

She wasn't a fussy sort, but this was intolerable. Ten nights sleeping in this floating barn? She could not do it.

She held her handkerchief to her nose. "What sort of animal bedded down here?"

"Goats and sheep," a porter muttered as he passed through the narrow hallway.

Abigail got a sinking feeling that couldn't be seasickness. They hadn't even left Boston harbor.

"This is disgusting," Miss Peabody exclaimed. "I've never seen such filth. To think I'd complained about my stateroom's bolsters in first class. You might as well be sleeping in a stable. I hope there are no vermin. If you catch a case of bedbugs or lice, I won't allow you on the stagecoach once we get to Galveston."

"Perhaps I should stay in Boston," Abigail offered again. "You won't even miss me. Or at least not once you get to Texas."

"I would very much miss you. *Especially* when I get to Texas. If you didn't want to come along, you shouldn't have urged me to become a mail-ordered bride. And you shouldn't have encouraged me by helping me write the letters." She pouted, sticking out her lower lip. "You can't leave me. Not now."

A pang of guilt squeezed Abigail's heart. It wasn't long ago that Miss Peabody sat at her parlor desk, holding the letter from Texas, completely lost as to how to respond. Abigail had only wanted to help and had suggested a few thoughts while Miss Peabody scribbled furiously.

Having never been courted herself, Abigail felt quite awkward offering advice. At nineteen, all she knew was how to be a companion for Miss Peabody. The gentleman from Texas, Mr. Walker, was twenty-eight years old and probably far more worldly. He was a wealthy rancher and she had the impression he was well-educated with a short military career. What could a simple girl like her have to say to a man like Mr. Walker?

Miss Peabody soon came to depend on Abigail's help with the letters. To her surprise, Abigail began to enjoy the letter-writing as well, spending long afternoons in the Peabody parlor, letting her mind wander with notions of romance and love. She wasn't sure how many of her ideas made it into the letters, for Miss Peabody kept the letters to herself, but she had fun, more fun than she'd had in many years.

"I won't leave you. Not if you need me."

"Good. That's settled then. I need to go back up. I can barely breathe down here. Are you coming?"

"If you don't mind, I want to take a moment or two to tidy up. I won't be long."

"Fine, but come soon. I need you to unpack my bags."

As Miss Peabody turned for the stairs, Abigail studied the hay-strewn floor. She'd have to scour the floors and walls. Maybe she could wrest the window open to coax a little fresh air into the dank rooms. The sea breeze would dispel the musty animal odors.

She felt suddenly tired. So very tired.

She didn't want to sweep. Or scour. Or sail to Texas.

She'd rather run away from it all. To bolt off the ship, down the pier and back to the crowded streets of the only town she'd ever known. Anything to avoid sailing all the way to Texas. The notion filled her with dread and sadness.

She'd promised to go, however, and couldn't abandon Miss Peabody.

Years ago, she'd made another promise, to Miss Peabody's parents, that she would care for Miss Peabody until she married. That was four long years ago. She never imagined Miss Peabody would be so hard to marry off. Suitors had come and gone. The last one offered marriage but that ended badly. Very badly.

As time passed, the circumstances for Miss Peabody had become more and more grim, and had now come to this – acceptance of a marriage proposal from a man in Texas who she'd never met, a wealthy rancher, supposedly, who needed a wife to help raise his nephew. Miss Peabody had been overjoyed at the offer. She wanted to leave at once. Anything to escape the sneers of the well-to-do of Boston.

Abigail moved to the nearest window and searched for a latch. Just then the ship lurched. At the base of the stairs, Miss Peabody stumbled and shrieked. Abigail cried out in pain.

"We're sinking," Miss Peabody shouted. "We're doomed. I knew I should never have stepped foot on a ship. Not after what happened to poor Grandpapa. It's the Peabody Curse!"

Abigail moved quickly to Miss Peabody's side.

"It's fine," Abigail said soothingly. "It's likely nothing more than a wave striking the hull."

"Are you certain? How can you be certain? What if it's a storm?"

"It can't be a storm. We just boarded and there wasn't a cloud in the sky."

Her employer rested a hand against her brow and moaned pitifully. Abigail wished she could convince Miss Peabody to go above board and rest her nerves. If she had a quarter hour, Abigail could make the rooms presentable for herself and the other passengers she expected to be along momentarily. Abigail wanted to spare them the sight of the dirty accommodations.

"I feel faint," Miss Peabody moaned.

"Let's go up and I will ask the porter to send tea. We won't set sail for another hour. Maybe two. We would have time before supper."

"That might help."

Abigail took her elbow and helped her up the stairs. Miss Peabody was not a small woman, not like Abigail. When another wave came along, Miss Peabody almost knocked Abigail over. By the time they reached the deck, Abigail was worn out, both from the effort of helping her mistress and having to listen about all manner of impending disaster.

"I told Mr. Walker he was lucky indeed. I'm not keen on ships, you know."

"I do know, in fact. You've mentioned that very fact to me in the past. Ten minutes ago."

"Cheeky girl. You're lucky too. I could have left you behind in Boston. Instead, I'm taking you along so you can help with the Walker baby, Jason."

"His name is Justin. Not Jason."

"Yes, well, it's a good thing I'm so magnanimous and insisted on taking you with me. You won't have to suffer through another miserable winter. And it's also a good thing that I come from such an upstanding family. Mr. Walker insisted his wife come from good stock. He won't marry some nobody. He was delighted that my family is so well-regarded."

Abigail pressed her lips together to keep from saying a word. While she would never dare to read Miss Peabody's private letters, she was sure Mr. Walker had emphasized his strong desire for a loving mother for his nephew. To Abigail's knowledge, at no point did Mr. Walker mention family name or reputation as a concern. A wife was a necessity, but the marriage was to be one of convenience.

Miss Peabody had told her as much when she'd received the man's first letter, which arrived exactly one month after the Reginald Penobscot debacle.

Reginald, Miss Peabody's former intended, had a change of heart the day they were to wed. Abigail cringed inwardly at the memory. While Miss Peabody could be tiring, no one deserved such humiliation.

When Miss Peabody decided to accept the offer of matrimony from the Texan, Abigail resolved to accompany Miss Peabody to her new home. Abigail had no intention of staying in Texas. Once her mistress was settled with her new husband, Abigail would take the next ship back to Boston.

She walked with Miss Peabody along the deck.

"Would you like to take in the view for a spell?" Abigail asked. She motioned to a bench that sat in a sunny spot away from the bustling crowds. "I could speak to the staff about some tea."

"Yes. That would do me some good. My rheumatism is troubling me. Yet another reason I'll be glad to see the shores of Texas."

Miss Peabody had sundry and numerous ailments, so many that at times she forgot the names and symptoms. For that reason, she kept a list of her complaints tucked in her bodice. Other times she easily remembered her maladies. That afternoon, for instance, she'd rattled off the top five conditions to the porter after he had the nerve to comment on the weight of her medicine valise.

Abigail left her mistress on the bench. Somewhere she was sure to find a member of the first class waitstaff.

She took a moment to admire the harbor. Pausing at the railing, she drew a deep breath, taking in the scent of the ocean. The sea breezes blew her hair loose. The sun shone on the water. In the distance, she spied several sailing ships.

Looking down, she saw the throng of people working their way to the ship. All manner of people were on the dock, some young, some old, some clearly there to see off loved ones. But then, for a moment, she thought she saw the very large ears of a certain Mr. Reginald Penobscot.

She scanned the crowd again, looking for the oversized ears. Was he there or not? The easiest way to spot him was to look at ears. The man had the largest ears she'd ever seen. She was sure he could hear conversations in Philadelphia.

She searched for the ears once more. She rose to her tiptoes, leaning against the railing, shielding her eyes from the midday sun. A moment ago, she could have sworn she saw him sauntering along the pier. Now he was gone. She gritted her teeth. How she disliked the man.

After a few moments she gave up, deciding that the sunlight glimmering off the surface of the ocean had tricked her, and had given her a start for no good reason. Reginald would be the *last* person to come to the dock. She'd heard that he set off for Canada to seek a fortune in the fishing trade. And good riddance, she'd thought at the time. The memory of Miss Peabody's heartbreak made her clench her fists. Many a time she'd imagined giving the scoundrel a piece of her mind.

Abigail resumed her search for a pot of hot tea. The ship was busy as a hive with all the comings and goings of the crew, passengers and those who had come to say their farewells. Finally, Abigail found the captain's orderly, who eyed her request with a haughty expression. Clearly, he thought her below his attention with her ragged boots and threadbare muslin dress.

"Her name's Miss Peabody," Abigail said.

He rolled his eyes. "You don't say. My name's Miss Peabody too. Blimey, there's a coincidence for ya."

His companions roared with laughter.

Abigail refused to let him rile her. She pointed to the papers in his hand. "You'll find her on the passenger list, in the very best quarters *The Sparrow* offers. Cabin 16."

The man grumbled as he sifted through the ship records. He drew a sharp breath. His brows lifted. "Awright, I'll have the tea along shortly."

"Thank you kindly," she said, keeping a polite tone.

Abigail made her way back to Miss Peabody, laughing at herself for thinking Reginald Penobscot was anywhere near this ship. It was impossible that Mr. Penobscot had heard of Miss Peabody's plans. Miss Peabody had told others about her upcoming nuptials, to be sure, but the well-to-do of Boston had dismissed her words.

Abigail was certain the news hadn't left the parlors of Boston's wealthy families. No one seemed to care about Miss Peabody. Or perhaps they didn't believe her. As she neared Miss Peabody's bench, however, her eyes fell on the ears of the very man she did not wish to see.

Mr. Penobscot, red-faced and blubbering, knelt at the feet of Miss Peabody.

# Chapter Two

**Caleb Walker**

The rain fell from the heavens as if the good Lord was pouring bucketsful. Caleb glanced at the steel-gray clouds and grimaced. No chance of a break in the storm. If anything, the wind blew colder, chilling him to the bone.

"I bet you're every bit as cold as I am, aren't you, Decker?" He leaned over in his saddle and pet the roan gelding's neck. The horse's coat held a dull shine in the fading daylight. Caleb made a note to rub the horse down and give him a hot mash when they returned to the barn. With any luck it would be before dark and not after.

He trotted across an arroyo. Decker's hooves splashed in the muddy rivulets as Caleb's mind wandered to his bride-to-be. Harriet Peabody.

Funny how he couldn't imagine calling her Harriet. In his letters, he always addressed her as Miss Peabody. Maybe it would always be Miss Peabody. Not that it would matter too much. The lady was coming a long way to help care for Justin and he'd call her however she wanted to be addressed. Formal. Informal. It didn't much matter to him.

The one thing he felt sure of was that he wouldn't use any sort of endearment. She wouldn't invite that sort of attention. Neither would he.

Their marriage was a business arrangement, plain and simple. She'd made sacrifices by coming all this way, but he'd made sacrifices too. Namely, a substantial sum of money.

In her first letter, she'd told him she had some debts she needed to settle. He realized that had to be one of the big reasons she sought a husband with money. To pay off family debts. He agreed and sent the funds. In the second letter, she claimed she needed a new wardrobe for the new life in Texas. He sent that too. Finally, she asked for additional travel funds for her maid.

Her maid?

At that point he began to wonder what he'd gotten himself into. Maybe the entire scheme was a bad idea. Maybe he didn't need anyone. He didn't question his need for a bride for long though. A day after that letter, he had to fire his fourth nanny when he smelled liquor on her breath.

He knew he needed a mother for the boy. Little Justin's crying was more than he could bear. The sound plum near broke his heart, especially when he couldn't do a thing to comfort the poor little mite. He needed a wife, one that would sign a marriage contract if she was suitable. The contract would keep her bound to her duty to the family.

It might not be fair, but life wasn't fair. If anyone doubted that point, they could ask little Justin how fair or unfair life could be.

Thunder rolled across the darkening sky. "Well, where do you think we might find this pesky foal, Decker?"

He'd been out for several hours which was why he'd resorted to talking to his horse. Things were grim, indeed. Too bad the gelding couldn't talk back.

The horse pricked his ears and whickered. In the din of the rain, Caleb thought he heard a faint reply. He urged his mount into a trot, moving toward a clump of grass on the far side of the arroyo. There, sprawled in knee high grass, he found the pitiful animal, half-dead and thoroughly soaked.

Caleb slipped from the saddle, crouched by the foal's side and ran his hands over its sodden coat. The foal tried to raise his head but couldn't manage more than a feeble motion.

"Easy there, little fellow," Caleb muttered. He gathered the animal in his arms and lifted him to the saddle. A moment later he was mounted behind the foal and they were on their way back to the stable.

A half hour later they arrived at his barnyard. His foreman, William, met him in the doorway of the barn. A look of disbelief lit his haggard expression. He shook his head. "You jus' don't give up, do you, boss?"

Caleb brushed the man's words aside with a casual shrug. "It was Decker who found him. Third time this year. Starting to think he's part bloodhound."

Easing the foal off the saddle, Caleb gathered him in his arms and carried him to the mare's stall. After they rubbed him with a rag, Caleb lifted him to his feet to nurse. The foal swayed unsteadily but was plenty hungry. He began to nurse, flicking his tail as he fed. The mare murmured softly and when the youngster finished, she skimmed her muzzle along the foal's withers.

Caleb watched a little longer from the stall door. The foal wandered unsteadily to a fresh pile of straw. He folded his long ungainly legs, lowered to his bed and settled down for a long nap. A moment later the mare lay down beside him. It wasn't long before the little one was fast asleep, nestled next to his doting mama.

Caleb tended to his own horse, feeding him and giving him a good rubdown too. Dusk gave way to darkness. The rain continued to fall but softer now. The thunder sounded in the distance.

Hungry, cold and tired, he decided it was time to call it a night. He bid his foreman good night and headed to the ranch house. His Aunt Eleanor waited for him in the dining room. She took one look at him and sent him upstairs to change out of his wet clothes.

Eleanor often traveled from her home in Houston to stay with him, especially now that he had a nephew to care for. Eleanor raised him and his twin brother after his mother and father perished in a hotel fire while visiting New Orleans.

Caleb and Andrew, his brother, were only six when his parents died, two rambunctious boys arriving on the doorstep of her grand home. By the end of the first day, he and Andrew had broken a vase and chipped the corner off her grandfather clock. Eleanor had to lay down the law. She often returned to her imperious ways when she came to visit.

When Andrew passed four months ago, Eleanor began regular, longer visits to the ranch. She took on the role of caretaker once more and presided over his home like the commanding officer of a military camp.

Her cane wasn't just for walking. It came in handy when she wanted to make a point. She'd bang the silver tip against the floor with a sharp rap to make her feelings known.

Upstairs, he stripped out of his wet, dirty work clothes, washed and put on a dry, clean set of pants and shirt. Before he went back down, he paused at the bedroom door of his nephew.

While Caleb was far from an expert on babies or children, he always wanted to make sure the boy was safe. Each night he'd listen at the door. He drew comfort from the sound of the child's soft breathing. He never ventured into the room for fear that he'd wake the child. From experience he knew, waking a sleeping baby was something to avoid if at all possible.

The child always rested a little better when Aunt Eleanor visited. Still, she often had trouble settling the little one for the night. Eleanor had a gentle touch. Despite her soft, kind ways with the baby, she could only do so much caretaking on account of her injured leg.

The boy needed a mama. And he needed her yesterday.

He needed love and consoling. The poor child never even met his father and lost his mother when he was only a day old. Both his parents had fallen ill from influenza and died.

Caleb had received word that his brother, who was a doctor, had fallen sick. By the time Caleb arrived in Austin, his brother was dead. His sister-in-law clung to life, barely. She hung on just long enough to bring Justin into the world. A day later she was dead.

The memory felt like a shard of glass in Caleb's heart. He'd dearly loved his brother and sister-in-law. Even though Andrew was his twin, the two were nothing alike. Still, Caleb missed him terribly. It seemed impossible Andrew was gone. As much as Caleb grieved his brother, he knew his loss paled by comparison to that of the baby. The poor child had very nearly joined his parents in death.

For the first few weeks of his life, the baby alternated between crying endlessly and sleeping a deep, unnatural rest.

Caleb felt the weight of caring for the boy as if it rested square on his heart. He vowed to do right by their child no matter what. Even if it meant taking a marriage of convenience.

At twenty-eight, he should have taken a wife long ago. Instead, he'd worked his ranch, making his fortune with cattle.

He'd intended to marry along the way, but there were so few women in Sweet Willow.

He'd considered courting a young lady in Houston. The refined ladies from the city didn't give a fig for a life in the wilds of Texas. Many of them flat-out refused to care for a stranger's child. Houston girls assumed they would have help to care for their *own* children.

He heaved a heavy sigh and dragged his hand across his jaw. When he was certain the boy was sleeping peacefully, he went downstairs. He sat at the head of the table. Aunt Eleanor fussed, complaining about catching a cold.

Caleb smiled as she served him a bowl of steaming soup. "I can't stay inside just on account of a little rain. Not when there's a lost foal."

"What about the rest of your family? Don't we count?" She grumbled and passed him the breadbasket.

"Yes, ma'am. You matter the most." *Especially the boy.*

He didn't need to tell her about his feelings for the child, though.

Family was important to Eleanor too. She'd been devastated when his brother died. For days, she hardly left her bed. It was only when Caleb went to her home in Houston and told her that he needed her help, and Justin needed her help too, that she pulled herself together.

His heartfelt, impassioned words roused her from her grief. She rose from her bed and embarked on a campaign of setting things to rights. She consoled herself with planning his life as Justin's father. She felt certain she knew what was best for both Caleb and Justin, and she let Caleb know just that several times a day every time she came to visit.

He also knew she wasn't done lecturing him. She'd arrived that morning fit to be tied on account of his plans to marry a mail-order bride.

She wasted no time getting straight to the point. "If your family matters the most, why not marry one of the nice girls I've mentioned?"

Aunt Eleanor gave him a prim look, daring him to argue. She folded her hands in front of her, clearly preparing to settle in for a nice long chat. "Lizbeth Doyle told me you wouldn't even come into town to take her to the symphony."

"I don't want to complain about Lizbeth or any of the girls you've introduced me to in Houston. They're all plenty nice."

"And cultured."

"That too."

"And very pretty."

"Yes, ma'am. They are."

"But?"

Caleb's shoulders tensed. "Not one of them seems interested in meeting Justin. They act like he'd be some sort of burden. The dark-haired gal, Cassie, wrinkled her nose like she'd stepped in something. Then the short, plump one, think her name was Katherine. She suggested sending him to an orphanage."

Aunt Eleanor blinked. For a long moment, she didn't respond. When she did, the sound came like a gust of winter wind. "You're exaggerating! Surely."

He shook his head. "Afraid not."

His aunt rubbed her forehead with dainty fingertips. A soft sigh came from her lips. She took a moment to compose herself. Even though she dearly wanted him to marry a girl of her choosing, she couldn't argue in favor of anyone who would send Justin off to an orphanage. Eleanor loved the boy, worried about him and thought only of his care.

When she spoke, it was in a soft, resigned tone. "A mail-order bride can't possibly be suitable. She most likely is taking your offer because she's poor and homely and unpleasant."

"Her last name is Peabody. Her great-grandfather started Peabody Shipping."

He drew some satisfaction in the way his aunt's brows lifted. There was more to the Peabody story – Miss Peabody's uncle had absconded with the family fortune, but Eleanor didn't need all the details. What mattered was that Eleanor was impressed. Clearly.

He neglected to mention anything about Miss Peabody's requests for money. Eleanor would not take kindly to that sort of opportunism. What difference did it make? He had plenty of money. Once the two of them were joined in holy matrimony, he would share everything he owned. He'd make certain to take care of his wife so that she'd take care of his nephew.

His heartbeat quickened to think that his bride-to-be had boarded a ship that very morning. A shimmer of anticipation moved inside his chest. It was foolish to have any feelings for a woman he didn't know, yet there it was. They had a business arrangement, and yet there were times where he felt sure her sweet letters softened a hard spot in his heart.

He didn't dare confess Miss Peabody's imminent travel plans to his aunt. It was better this way. Aunt Eleanor would have a fit if she knew the girl was about to embark on her voyage to Texas. It would be far better to let Eleanor think that the mail-order bride was just an idea he was mulling over.

His aunt drummed her fingers on the linen tablecloth, a faraway look in her eyes. "Peabody, eh?"

"You know the name?"

"No. But I'm not troubled that I haven't heard of the girl's family. While I'm acquainted with everyone worth knowing in Texas, I don't know many people in Boston." She lifted her nose and sniffed. Then she fixed her gaze on Caleb, narrowing her eyes. "I'll know everything if I meet her one day. I'm an excellent judge of character. She won't be able to hide any secrets from me."

"No," he replied. "No, ma'am."

Caleb kept from smiling at his aunt's stern threat. No one could hide anything from Aunt Eleanor. Not for long.

# Chapter Three

**Abigail**

The sight of Mr. Penobscot sparked a deep burning resentment inside Abigail's heart. The cad. The scoundrel. The jilter! Was here on *The Sparrow*!

While Abigail dearly wanted to see Miss Peabody married off, she also needed to know the union would be a happy one. Miss Peabody could be persnickety. Not all men would find her demanding ways to be endearing.

Abigail gritted her teeth as her protective instincts took hold. Miss Peabody stared at her former suitor with stunned astonishment. Abigail called for the crew to remove the trespasser. Mr. Penobscot gaped as well, his red, flushed face turning pale when several burly crew members hurried to the scene.

"I insist on speaking to Miss Peabody," he shouted.

"You had your chance, sir," Abigail shouted back.

A murmur of dismay came from bystanders. Abigail's face heated. She didn't want to create a scene but needed to shield Miss Peabody from the man who had caused her so much suffering.

Miss Peabody said nothing. She slumped over on the bench, clutching the armrest for dear life. The only sound coming from the woman was a small murmur of dismay as she gawked at her former fiancé.

More passengers and crew gathered to watch the unfolding drama. Abigail flushed with embarrassment, for herself as well as Miss Peabody, but she refused to relent.

"Remove this man," Abigail demanded. "He is a scoundrel and a menace and a..." Her words failed her as she wracked her brain for the proper description. In her mind, she could still picture poor Miss Peabody, dressed in her wedding gown, sobbing while gazing mournfully at the silver trays piled with petit fours.

Penobscot had promised her the moon. In the end, he hadn't even sent a note to call the wedding off. Abigail's indignation burned even hotter at the memory.

"He is not a passenger on this ship." She didn't know if that was true or not, but that seemed to be the surest way to get the crew engaged. "And he's a liar, too!" Abigail added, her voice shaking.

The crowd gasped. Several of the older ladies murmured disparaging remarks about Mr. Penobscot. Each comment drew a cry of distress from Miss Peabody, who fanned herself with her handkerchief.

Mr. Penobscot looked at Abigail pleadingly as if begging her not to heap any more fury upon his balding head.

Abigail would not relent, however. The wedding day still burned in her memory. Miss Peabody stood at the altar for over an hour, assuring everyone that her darling Reginald was simply late, trying to make everything perfect for their wedding day. Of course, he never showed, nor sent word of any kind.

The day had been a disaster. An outrage. A scandalous story that Abigail suspected still made the rounds in the fine homes of Boston.

To think the rogue had come to the ship! Why? To plead his case?

She moved closer to deliver her strongest accusation. She lifted a hand and pointed a shaking finger at the man. "That man is a heartbreaker!"

With that, Miss Peabody began to sob. A collective murmur of complaint moved across the growing crowd. The crew stepped closer, each man glaring at the intruder. Mr. Penobscot looked as if he might join Miss Peabody, who lay on the bench in a rather inelegant, sniffling heap.

"It was a mistake," Mr. Penobscot said, his voice trembling. "A mistake I shall rue until the day I die. I've returned for a second chance. I'm ready for marriage now that I've made my fortune." He looked around as if trying to appeal to the crowd. "I've made a mint. Fishing. In Canada. They call me the King of Cod."

A few of the men in the crowd nodded. Most of the women still looked outraged on Miss Peabody's behalf. The crew looked uncertain.

Abigail fretted that her support might be faltering. She refused to let Mr. Penobscot gain a foothold amongst the passengers and crew. Mr. Walker waited for Miss Peabody in Texas. A good, noble man who wouldn't abandon her at the altar to go fishing in Canada.

"I see no reason to believe you," Abigail fumed. With her poor mistress lying helplessly in plain view, her fury only grew deeper. She took a step closer toward Mr. Penobscot, wishing she could somehow shield Miss Peabody from the crowd and from him as well. He retreated a step and then another, a small whimper spilling from his lips.

"You have no right to come here. Not on the day we're to depart for a new, wonderful life in Texas."

The women in the crowd murmured their agreement. A few of the men grumbled.

Abigail was a slight, young woman. A small detail she forgot anytime she encountered some form of injustice. She set her hands on her hips and closed the distance between herself and the pale, trembling man.

"You left this poor, innocent woman at the altar!"

A gasp came from the crowd.

Emboldened, Abigail went on. "Now get off this ship, or I shall have you thrown off."

Several of the women standing nearby chimed in. *That's it. Toss him off our ship. The nerve of the man leaving his bride at the altar.*

"Oye, ya heard the lady," one of the crew growled. "Be off or we'll show you off, won't we, lads?"

Before the rest of the crew could join in his threatening words, Mr. Penobscot turned on his heel. Without a backwards glance, he hurried across the deck. He scrambled down the gangplank, pausing on the dock to give one final look of longing at his ladylove. Abigail moved to the railing and shouted more words of warning. Women came to her side and offered their own threats and accusations.

*Be off, you cur... You don't deserve her... Or any girl...*

Mr. Penobscot rushed away, vanishing a moment later. His portly form disappeared into the bustling crowd. Abigail waited and watched, her heart pounding in her chest. She half-expected him to reappear and insist on speaking to Miss Peabody to beg her to reconsider.

"Well done, you," one of the women said to Abigail.

"I should say so," said another.

Abigail blushed. Her skin prickled uncomfortably as she realized she was the object of a fair bit of attention. Worse, the other passengers seemed overly interested in Miss Peabody, staring at the poor woman as she moaned on the bench.

"What's happening?" Miss Peabody murmured. "Where am I?"

Abigail pushed her way through the crowd and went to her side. She beckoned one of the crew to come help Miss Peabody back to her room. One of the bigger fellows picked up the stricken Miss Peabody.

"Oye, a little heavier than she appears," he muttered, wincing.

Abigail narrowed her eyes in warning.

The man's eyes widened. "Sorry, miss."

She set off, showing the man the way. Together they walked the length of the deck and went below to the first-class cabins. Cabin number 16 was grand and luxurious with several plush, overstuffed chairs and sofas.

The man plopped Miss Peabody rather unceremoniously on the chaise. She landed with a huff and proceeded to weep, loud sniffling sounds, punctuated with wails of grief.

The man hurried to the door as if worried he might get chided for his manners. Or perhaps he worried that he might hear more of Miss Peabody's sobs. He tipped his hat and slipped out the doorway with a few words of farewell and a brief mention of the ship's departure that evening before supper.

Miss Peabody's weeping quieted.

Abigail lay a blanket across her mistress's lap. She urged the woman to rest. Miss Peabody sank back with a plaintive moan. Abigail paced the cabin. Back and forth she strode, trying to make sense of the events.

Finally, she gave up her furious pacing and set about tidying the cabin.

She needed something to do. That would help calm her frantic thoughts.

She started with the trunks. One was filled to the brim with sweets, boxes and tins of candy, chocolates and the French bonbons Miss Peabody favored. Abigail frowned at the assortment and stole a glance at Miss Peabody's dress, straining at the seams. The woman snorted, tugged the blanket over her shoulder and turned on her side.

Abigail studied the collection of sweets and recalled the family doctor chiding Miss Peabody. He'd informed her in no uncertain terms that she should refrain from indulging in so many treats. The sweets were to blame for her stout figure. Miss Peabody had grown red in the face and almost speechless with indignation. When she recovered, she had railed against the doctor.

*I hardly eat a single sweet. Why, I eat like a bird. What could you mean to say that my figure is stout?*

Abigail considered hiding the sweets, but she knew it would do no good. Not unless she dragged the trunk to her quarters below. Her cabin seemed too dirty to store candy or any foods. The boxes of sweets might attract vermin. *Rats...*

Abigail got a little lightheaded at the thought of rats.

She prayed there weren't any rodents in the steerage class. There was nothing that frightened her more than rats. Two of the girls at the orphanage had been bitten by rats and nearly died from the fever. Even now, some years later, Abigail could picture the girls' swollen limbs and the gruesome infections.

She shuddered at the memory.

No, it wouldn't do to take a trunk full of sweets to her filthy cabin. Instead, she shut the lid, pushed the trunk into a corner and covered it with a linen tablecloth. If the sweets were out of sight, Miss Peabody might forget about them.

Next, she set out Miss Peabody's toiletries. The woman's dresses she hung in the wardrobe, but only had room for half. Her boots and shoes, she set neatly in the shoe closet. Finally, she laid out her mistress's pens, writing paper and envelopes. Her breath caught in her throat. Mr. Walker's letters lay amongst the fountain pens and ink, the missives tied with a ribbon.

Abigail had tied the small bundle of letters herself. She'd rescued the letters from the rubbish bin, thinking that one day Miss Peabody would be pleased to have them. She ran her fingers along the edges of the paper, wondering not for the first time about the man who waited for Miss Peabody.

From the beginning, Miss Peabody had needed help with her letters. She begged and whined for Abigail to give her the right words. And Abigail did her best. Miss Peabody seemed to write down every word, precisely as Abigail said them. Abigail wasn't sure, however. She might have only imagined that her words were the exact ones put down on the parchment and sent to Texas. She'd never know.

She tried not to think about the baby, Justin. Or Mr. Walker. Standing here with his letters in hand, she desperately wanted to sit down and read each one. But she could not. It would violate Miss Peabody's trust. She set the bundle of letters back in the box.

Miss Peabody had settled considerably and seemed to be dozing, which gave Abigail time to reflect. Her thoughts remained on Mr. Walker.

At first, she'd pictured the man as a southern version of Mr. Penobscot. Over time, her impression changed.

Miss Peabody would share small snippets of his letters. Mr. Walker struck Abigail as a hard-working man with plenty of money, or so it seemed from his talk of land and possessions and his love of fine horses. And yet, he seemed unconcerned with the matters of wealth. Not like Miss Peabody's friends and family who always went on about their latest trips or acquisitions or evenings at the theater.

Furtively, and with a thudding heart, Abigail picked up the letters again, raising them to sniff the paper. She felt foolish whenever she inhaled the scent of the letters, but that feeling of foolishness didn't keep her from breathing in the faintly spicy fragrance.

Closing her eyes, she let out a soft sigh. The letters always sent a thrill across her thoughts. She shivered. She was a practical girl, one who never dared hope for anything grand. Doing so only resulted in disappointment.

For years, she'd waited for her father and mother to return to the orphanage. Years. They'd left her at the orphanage when she was less than two. She had no memories of her parents, of course. Just letters. Over the years, Rachel and Jacob Winthrop had written three times to tell her of California and how they intended to return for her.

She'd been a young, foolish girl, with silly dreams of a family. Her hopes sustained her dreams until the last and final letter from California. The letter came from a pastor, telling of her parent's illness and subsequent passing.

All she had of her parents were the few letters. With their death, that small, fragile connection was broken, and with it, her dreams. From that point on, she made certain not to dream or hope for anything. It was far better to be practical, she'd learned over the years. She didn't waste time on hope.

When she was almost ten, the Peabody family had taken her in. They didn't offer her a place in their family, but they were kind to her, more generous than she ever expected. They valued her practical ways. In time, they even depended on her sensible nature.

Mr. Peabody praised her for her mind and regularly bought her novels from the bookshop. Mrs. Peabody valued her help and insights in running the home. By the time she was fourteen, Abigail took care of the household shopping and budget. Over the years, as they got older, both Mr. and Mrs. Peabody relied on her more and more. Now, they too were gone.

Abigail ran her fingers over the edge of Mr. Walker's letters, wondering if he had servants to tend to his home. She hoped so. Miss Peabody didn't know the first thing about running a household.

Behind her, Miss Peabody moaned and muttered something about pastries.

A rush of guilt swept over Abigail. She dropped the letters and turned away. Ever since he'd first written, she wondered what Mr. Walker had shared in his letters. Sweet tender words? Promises of romance? She dearly wanted to know but wouldn't allow herself to pry into Miss Peabody's affairs.

She was a practical girl, after all.

She left the cabin to tend to her own accommodations. She'd come back later, after Miss Peabody had a well-deserved rest. Leaving, she shut the door softly behind her.

The narrow hallway was filled with passengers and crew. She overheard one of the crew members telling a passenger the ship would leave in three hours. This gave her time to do a few of her own chores. While her mistress slept, she would tend to her own room. She rolled up her sleeves, determined to have it cleaned and scoured by the time the ship set sail.

# Chapter Four

**Caleb**

Usually, Aunt Eleanor stayed no longer than a few days. She didn't care for the ranch. She made no secret of that, and openly said she always hoped he would have chosen a different career. Ever since he was a boy, Eleanor had encouraged him to have a military career in the Navy.

Out of respect and the love he felt for his aunt, he'd served in the military for two years, but he didn't care for the sea. Or ships. Or seasickness. He was honorably discharged and purchased a ranch immediately after. His aunt simply had to accept that he needed to have his feet on solid ground.

He loved the land. He understood ranching and over the years built a fortune.

Eleanor never tried to get Andrew to join the military because his constitution was weaker, and not meant for such demanding work. Caleb was the strong one. At times, he'd felt guilty about his robust health while his twin brother seemed to get sick easily.

As people tend to do, Caleb found a way to blame himself for his brother's weak health. He'd been born first, by a matter of minutes. In his mind, he figured that he'd fought to be the first one out, and that somehow the struggle had weakened his brother, before they ever saw the light of day. He knew it wasn't reasonable to worry about that but worries seldom were reasonable. His heavy heart made him more determined to properly care for Justin. It was the very least he could do for the boy.

By the third day of his aunt's visit, Caleb realized she planned to stay a spell. A plan that suited him just fine. He wouldn't have to worry so much about the boy's care. Little Justin was being tended by a patchwork of Aunt Eleanor, the cook's sister and the upstairs maid.

Caleb disliked the fact that, yet again, the boy didn't have a single caretaker, but a patchwork of childminders. It seemed a poor arrangement. As expected, the boy fussed and fretted. Even Aunt Eleanor couldn't work her magic.

On Sunday morning, he hitched the buggy and took his aunt and nephew into Sweet Willow for services. The boy slept all way through the sermon and woke only when the pastor said his final blessing. As if on cue, Justin's eyes widened, and he began to howl.

Caleb hurried outside to spare the parishioners from the loud crying. Eleanor came as quickly as she could. She carried the basket with the bottle and diapers. After a few moments of fumbling, she tugged a bottle out of the depths of the basket and handed it to Caleb. The milk was cold, but it couldn't be helped.

The boy drank his bottle, his small brows knit with the same furious expression he always wore when he woke. An old fear, one he'd known all his life, squeezed Caleb's heart. Amidst his deepest worries, he fretted that maybe the boy wasn't well. What if the boy turned out to be as frail as Andrew?

Surely Justin's constitution was hale and hearty. Surely. Caleb rocked the boy as he drank his bottle. He was never entirely comfortable holding the boy, and sometimes Caleb thought that Justin could sense his unease. When he wasn't drinking his milk, Justin would often arch his body away from Caleb's embrace.

His thoughts drifted to Miss Peabody's letters. She'd included a passage about the innocence of a baby. How even a small, defenseless child had hopes and dreams tucked inside his tiny heart. In the business-like exchange of letters, that short passage had struck him with an unexpected surge of emotion.

She was the one.

The tender words inspired a deep yearning inside his heart. He had to bring Miss Peabody to Texas. Even if her debts required a king's ransom, he wanted her to be the one to care for the boy.

The parishioners filed out of church. They regarded him with a mix of pity and curiosity. A child's care was a woman's domain. He knew that and he wanted to tell them how he was perfectly aware that his attempts to tend to the boy were clumsy, at best.

He excelled at ranching, not caring for a baby.

For the past six years he'd worked tirelessly on his ranch. He'd bought the ranch at an excellent price and in the next few years tripled the acreage and holdings. Everything he touched brought him money. Other ranchers would have liked to marry their daughters to Caleb, but none suited him. None suited the boy.

Only the woman who had penned the letters would do for Justin.

Caleb drove the buggy home while Aunt Eleanor held the baby. The ride was mostly peaceful. His aunt seemed lost in thought.

"It's a beautiful day," he said idly.

"Isn't it, though?" She smiled broadly. An instant later she hiccupped.

He frowned. His aunt was a poor liar. He and his brother had determined that early on. Whenever she tried to coax them into a fitting for a new suit, or try piano lessons for the fifth time, she'd scheme and lie in wait to surprise them. She always gave herself away, however, by her small, inelegant hiccups. Margaret Walker was a straight arrow. Her conscience betrayed her plans every time.

He wondered what she might be concealing.

They drove up the hill, a pretty spot that showed off the extent of the Walker Ranch. A grove of majestic oaks surrounded his home. He'd rebuilt the home, using limestone so it would be sturdy and withstand the spring storms.

Usually, he liked to stop and admire the view. Not today. Irritation washed over him. His bride-to-be would arrive in a little over a few weeks' time. This was no time for his aunt's shenanigans.

"What is it, Aunt Eleanor?" he demanded.

She recoiled, giving him an indignant look. He supposed the look was meant to convey innocence. He almost fell for it, until she hiccupped again. Justin stirred in her arms. He yawned. His lids drooped.

"Shh," Eleanor whispered. "The little angel wants to sleep."

Caleb grumbled under his breath. His aunt was a sweet woman. A kind woman.

She was also forged of steel. She'd been widowed as a young woman. Childless and alone, she managed her late husband's mining interests, making a fortune by the time she was only thirty-five. A few years after, she sold her shares in the mine when she took Caleb and Andrew in to raise them as her own.

Eleanor was undoubtably a shrewd businesswoman, but she was a terrible liar.

He shook his head to let her know he wasn't buying any of it.

They continued down the road to the house. Caleb stopped the buggy at the front door. The cook, her assistant and the downstairs maid came to help his aunt and take the baby inside.

A gentle breeze blew, warm and fragrant.

"Ah, do you smell that?" Eleanor asked.

"I smell something all right," Caleb said, giving her a pointed look.

She gave him a bland smile before turning her attention to the road. A buggy traveled down the hillside, carrying two people. One person dressed in a dark suit sat beside a woman wearing a bright yellow dress.

"Oh, my," Eleanor said. She lifted her hand to wave, punctuating the gesture with a hiccup. "I wonder who that could be?"

Caleb leaned against the buggy. "Uh huh."

Aunt Eleanor drew back her shoulders to give him a chastising look. "Don't you uh-huh me, young man."

"Sorry, Aunt Eleanor. I meant to say that I wonder who it could be too, ma'am."

She beamed. Clearly, she felt certain she'd scored a point on some matter. "I believe it could be Clarence Worthington with his daughter. They must be passing through Sweet Willow. Clarence named his daughter Clarice. Isn't that lovely? Poor Clarence never had a son. He and his wife Enid struggled for years to have a child, and in the finish, the good Lord gave them a girl. Just one child. A girl child at that. Such a shame. No matter. He named his daughter after the female version of his own name. Which is Clarice. They're just in time for lunch and I just happen to have two extra places set at the table. Company. Out here. How charming."

Caleb studied his aunt, noting the way she rattled on and on.

He found it curious that Aunt Eleanor could tell that the people in the buggy way off on the hill were her friends from Houston. That seemed like a pretty uncanny guess from this distance. It also seemed like getting named after your father was a raw deal for the girl, but Caleb didn't want to point that out. "Yes. Charming. That's just what I was going to say."

Aunt Eleanor's smile faltered. She sighed heavily and lifted her gaze heavenward as if lost in heartfelt prayer. "Please, dear Lord. Remind Caleb that he and his brother, rest his soul, were the cause of my gray hair. Let my nephew recall *some* of the manners he learned at the military academy. I only ask this." She finished on a tearful note. "I pray my darling nephew will agree that's not too much to give a poor, elderly woman."

With that she wiped an imaginary tear from the corner of her eye and returned her attention to the approaching buggy, her determined smile once again gracing her lips.

# Chapter Five

**Abigail**

The steerage class was divided into men's quarters and women's quarters. The cabins below were filled to capacity as most of the passengers had boarded. The cabins in the aft were slated for female passengers and bustled with a hum of activity. Women searched for their quarters, some of them toting several trunks.

Despite the smell and mess, excitement filled the air. Soon the ship would set sail. By nightfall the ship would reach the open seas.

Abigail felt the air of excitement keenly. Up to now she'd dreaded the voyage, but everyone seemed excited to be aboard, and it filled her with anticipation. She was on a ship! Heading for adventure! This was nothing like anything she'd ever known.

When she returned to her cabin, she found other fellow passengers had arrived, a young woman and a girl who would share the dark, musty rooms.

"My name is Laura Ipswitch," the young woman said. "And this is Francine."

"Pleased to meet you," Abigail replied. "My name is Abigail Winthrop."

The girl looked to be about seven or eight. She averted her eyes and said nothing. "Francine has been a little quiet lately,"

Laura said. "Her mother passed several months ago. The two of us are heading to Texas for a fresh start."

Abigail was surprised at the revelation. A fresh start? She eyed the girl with curiosity and sympathy too. The poor child had lost her mother. Abigail wondered how, but it was clear that Laura had said all she intended to say on the subject.

Laura's demeanor was friendly, cheerful and matter of fact, a stark contrast to the melancholy young girl.

While Laura's nature was sweet and easygoing, she seemed entirely out of place among the second-class passengers. Dressed in a velvet-trimmed, blue frock, she looked as if she should be upstairs in first class. Francine wore a similar dress with fine lambskin boots. Abigail yearned to ask why the two of them had the misfortune of ending up below deck with her but didn't want to pry, just yet.

"I hoped to clean the room so it would be somewhat more comfortable," Abigail said. "I asked one of the crew to bring a bucket of soapy water."

Laura nodded her agreement. "The cabin is a sight. I'd intended to stay in quarters above board but had to pay for this extra little passenger." She wrinkled her nose with distaste as she looked around. "It seems the prior occupants were farm animals."

"They were goats and sheep, I've been told." Abigail smiled to see the look of shock and horror on Laura's face. Francine, on the other hand, looked as if she might smile at this bit of news.

Abigail felt dowdy next to Laura. A keen prickling awareness of her own simple clothes made her blush. She owned two dresses, both identical muslin frocks. The one she'd chosen to wear to board the ship was the more threadbare, but neither dress was near the quality of Laura's elegant dress.

Abigail was about to tell the girl that she would manage the cleaning, but Laura set to work before she could stop her. Laura took the bucket from Abigail and began to scrub the walls. Francine took a broom and began to sweep the hay. Over the next half hour, the two girls swept the hay and piled it in a corner in hopes the crew would remove it once the ship set sail.

Laura explained that she was on her way to Texas to become a mail-order bride. She had, in fact, worked with the same agency Miss Peabody had used, Massachusetts Matchmakers. The company was known for placing well-born ladies with discriminating gentlemen in the west.

They worked as they spoke. When Abigail finished scrubbing the walls, she got on her hands and knees to scour the floor. Laura didn't hesitate to help. Francine wrung out the dirty rags.

"All my life, I've worked as a seamstress," Laura said. "Mr. Bailey thought that spoke well of me. He wrote that I'd make myself useful because I could sew his shirts and trousers as well as run his household."

She grinned and blew a lock of hair from her eyes. "Not exactly romantic. He seems to have some money, or I assume so if he contracted with a matchmaking agency. Still, I suspect he chose me because he might save a few pennies on his tailoring. Not for walks in the moonlight."

Abigail doubted that. Laura was a pretty young woman. With long blonde hair and wide blue eyes, she looked like an angel. Abigail glanced at the little girl. Francine worked quietly wiping the cobwebs from the corners. The little girl was lovely too, but her dark hair and eyes didn't favor Laura.

"Francine isn't my child," Laura said quietly, guessing her thoughts. "Her mother worked as a seamstress in the same shop I worked for. I've known Francine since she was a baby. When her mother passed, I took her in. The girl hasn't spoken a word since her mother passed. I went to the matchmaking agency so the two of us could have a fresh start away from the sad memories. I didn't want to place her in an orphanage. Especially not the Mill Street Home."

Abigail recoiled at the name of the orphanage. "I'm glad you didn't take her there. I lived there as a child."

Laura drew a sharp breath.

Abigail brushed off her worries. "I left a long time ago."

"Your parents died?" Laura's face pinked. "I'm sorry. I have a terrible habit of speaking before I think."

"My mother and father put me in the orphanage, intending to come for me when they could. They set off for California so my father could find work as a stonemason. I was told they wrote several times, sending money and promising to come for me upon their return."

Abigail didn't mention her foggy, nagging memories of her family. The director of the orphanage once mentioned there was another child. Her parents had taken that child with him. Over the years, Abigail's mind rejected the notion of a brother or sister. It couldn't be. Why would her parents take one child and leave the other?

"And then what happened?" Laura asked.

"They never returned. I discovered later that they'd died on their way back."

"Dear heavens."

"Not long after, I was taken to live with a very nice family," Abigail said lightly. She never liked to be viewed with pity. "Does Mr. Bailey know about the little one?" she asked.

"Not yet," Laura said. "I hope to convince him that I couldn't leave her behind." She batted her lashes. "I'll use my feminine charms if need be."

Abigail couldn't help smiling at Laura's confidence. How lucky for Francine that she had such a kind-hearted young lady to care for her. Surely the man in Texas, Mr. Bailey, would take them both.

Surely.

# Chapter Six

**Caleb**

Aunt Eleanor settled in as if she intended to stay a while. She ordered the meals, instructed Justin's caretakers and made sure things ran according to her plan.

Fortunately, her plan did not include any more unexpected guests. The fellow who had arrived with his daughter didn't stay more than a quarter hour before leaving. His daughter made no secret of her disinterest. The ranch hadn't been up to her standards. She'd left in a snit, her behavior troubling even to Eleanor, who didn't bother inviting anyone else.

Caleb and Eleanor settled into an uneasy truce.

She might have given up inviting debutantes, but she still fretted he might make a careless choice of bride and mother for Justin. She shadowed his every move as if suspecting that he might sneak off and exchange vows with a secret bride he had hidden away. When he headed out with his men at dawn, she came to the porch to wave them off. She probably searched the group of men for a glimpse of a petticoat.

His men, especially the old-timers, knew that his Aunt Eleanor liked to fuss over him. They relished how the boss, a great big cowboy who could wrestle a yearling calf to the ground, had to answer to his elderly aunt. They'd joke about it. Usually behind his back. Lately they hadn't bothered to conceal their amusement and flat-out give him grief about the *lady-boss.*

In a way, Caleb wished his aunt could stay and take care of things. She directed the help in the kitchen and oversaw the maids and the patchwork of care he had for the boy. He knew, however, that caring for the house and the boy tired her. She refused to rest her injured leg and carried on as if she was a woman half her age. By the end of each day, she was pale and exhausted.

At the end of the first week of her visit, one of his men told Caleb there was a fence down in the back pastures. Usually, that was something his men could take on without him. The problem lay in what was beyond the fence, a particularly troublesome neighbor. A man he'd feuded with in the past.

Seth Bailey.

The man owned a ranch almost as big as Caleb's. The size of his arrogance matched his holdings. Not only that, he seemed to enjoy making a mountain out of a molehill. If there was a problem with the fence, Caleb could depend on locking horns with Seth.

He took several of his best men and rode to the back pastures. Sure enough, he found Seth riding the length of fence line, inspecting the stretch for signs of mischief no doubt. Caleb gritted his teeth when he saw that Seth had brought his brother, Noah.

"Good morning," Caleb said as he drew near.

"Easy for you to say," Seth replied. "It seems your men are trying to move the fence line onto my property."

Caleb eyed the posts and wire. They lay scattered across the ground as if someone had, indeed, knocked them down. It was a good thing he didn't have any cattle roaming in the back pastures. He didn't need any of his cattle on Bailey land. That had happened a time or two in the past and Caleb had battled mightily to retrieve his animals.

He resented the implication that his men were guilty of some wrongdoing. Fences got knocked down all the time. And not necessarily by men. Cattle could be plenty destructive. Especially Longhorns. In the past, he wouldn't hesitate to tangle with Seth Bailey. There was a time he sort of liked a good brawl. But he was a father now. And he had a wife on the way, and Caleb suspected Miss Peabody wouldn't approve of his brawling ways.

"I'm sure we can settle this without a fight," Caleb said, attempting an amiable tone.

Seth scoffed. "I know you, Walker. You wouldn't hesitate to take what's mine."

Caleb felt his shoulders tighten a notch. Those were fighting words if ever he heard them. Even Seth's brother looked a tad surprised.

Noah Bailey drew close, riding the dun gelding he always favored. His brow lifted, a sign that his brother's words struck him as harsh. With that one, it wasn't always easy to tell, Caleb decided long ago. While Seth was loud and argumentative, Noah was quiet and thoughtful.

"Say what you will about me, Bailey," Caleb replied easily. "The property lines were drawn long ago. All we need to do is take a look at the deed."

Seth knit his brows. Now it was his turn to be surprised. In the past, Caleb would have taken offense at the slight and responded with an insult of his own. Noah's lips twitched with a ghost of a smile. Sometimes Caleb thought he liked the younger brother more, or perhaps he disliked him less.

"What you say," Seth drawled, "we just sit ourselves down in your parlor for some tea and cookies, and talk it over all gentleman-like?"

"Sounds fine to me." Caleb offered a wry grin. "I'll put the kettle on."

He heard his own men mutter behind him. If they'd given him grief about his aunt bossing him around, he'd hear no end to their complaints about Seth Bailey. Not that Caleb had any intention of having a friendly talk with his troublesome neighbor. He just didn't want to fight every time he saw the man. These days he had more than himself to think about.

"Fences don't last forever, you know that. This one's down and I'm offering to pay to rebuild it. On the property line. Let's look at the deed and agree where that is. Okay?"

Seth frowned. Clearly, he too expected different. He studied the fence line once more. Slowly he drew off his cowboy hat, rested it on his pommel and scratched his head. "I suppose I could check the deed."

He returned his worn cowboy hat to his head and regarded Caleb with what looked like a more relaxed expression. The hard line of his mouth softened. His hands gripped the reins a little less tightly.

Caleb blinked, hardly believing that Seth could say words that seemed almost conciliatory.

The early morning haze drifted overhead. The sun broke through a thin veil of mist and lit the surrounding pastures. The sunshine chased the chill from the morning air and for some reason brightened Caleb's mood a little more. Maybe this was a good sign.

"I have a wife coming," Caleb said gruffly. "A mail-ordered wife from Boston. I have no use for a feud with anyone, much less a neighbor."

Seth peered at Caleb from the brim of his hat. The fire had returned to his eyes. He pressed his lips to form a thin line once more. Even Noah looked perturbed. He turned his head and spat.

"You trying to get my goat?" Seth demanded.

Caleb, for the life of him, couldn't imagine what he might have done to offend the man now. Seth Bailey was impossible. He'd known that from their first meeting at a Sweet Willow horse auction. Caleb had outbid him on a fine stud horse and Seth hadn't ever forgiven him. The man was as prickly as a porcupine. He'd argue with a fencepost.

"I'm not trying to get your goat, or your property." Caleb tried to school his tone so that Seth wouldn't somehow find offense with that too. "I'm simply trying to suggest we get along. You know? Be neighborly."

Seth turned his ire on his brother. "You going around town talking about my business?"

Noah curled his lip. He didn't reply but his expression said it all. Caleb still had no idea what had gotten into Seth Bailey. He turned in his saddle to glance back at his men. They too looked perplexed. William, his foreman, shrugged.

"What's the trouble now, Bailey?" Caleb demanded, his patience wearing thin.

"I don't take kindly to you making remarks about mail-ordered brides. I'd like to know where you heard I had one coming?"

Caleb let out a huff of surprise. Seth Bailey couldn't have come up with anything more astonishing. He might as well have said that he expected the Queen of England.

"I hadn't heard," Caleb said slowly.

"Sure about that?"

"Not a word."

Noah shook his head. Seth seemed to mull over Caleb's words for a few moments before he had the sense to look a little sheepish. He shrugged and gave his brother what might have suggested a look of apology.

"A man needs sons to carry on his name," Seth said.

"I happen to be waiting on a mail-order bride as well." Caleb glanced over his shoulder. As he could have guessed, his men stared with eyes big as silver dollars. "Not a word. Understand?"

The men nodded in unison.

"Bad idea," Noah muttered. "Those women write about being young, innocent pretty little things, but that ain't what's stepping off the boat."

The words were some of the very few words that Caleb had ever heard come from Noah's lips. They sounded grim. Very grim. Noah's faint smile gave way to a wry grin.

Noah continued, "the two of you are going to wind up with a couple of misfit wives. Bow-legged. Gap-toothed. Probably with a few brats in tow."

Caleb gritted his teeth. Noah never spoke and here he was offering a veritable speech. It aggravated him to no end that the man was suggesting something so disrespectful of Miss Peabody. Or any woman.

Even Seth looked mad as a hornet's nest. Caleb didn't need to look over his shoulder to know that his men probably sat on their horses, slack jawed. They'd probably ridden out with him in hopes of a good fistfight. A man just needed to blow off a little steam every now and then. There wasn't going to be a brawl, and to top it off, they were having a chat about womenfolk.

Caleb felt the need to defend the honor of Miss Peabody. He couldn't let Noah denigrate the woman, especially in front of his men. "That won't be the case," he said from between gritted teeth. "I went through a matchmaker."

Seth's eyes narrowed. "So did I."

A sudden and troubling thought came to Caleb. "Your bride's name isn't Miss Peabody, is it?"

He held his breath, waiting. If Seth said yes, they'd have a whole new fight on their hands and this one wouldn't involve a fence line. It would involve a woman.

Noah seemed to find the question amusing. He chuckled and shook his head. Seth glared at his brother and then turned his attention to Caleb. "Her name is not Miss Peabody. It's Laura Ipswitch. And she's a seamstress."

Noah nodded. "Sure, she is."

"Why don't you shut your mouth?" Seth shot back.

One of his men muttered. *A seamstress?*

The rest of the men joined in. A chorus of comments followed.

*We could use a seamstress... Ain't got one of them in Sweet Willow... Maybe she could mend my Sunday trousers...Wonder if she might sew a button...*

Fortunately, Seth didn't hear. He and Noah were bickering. The breeze stirred, making their argument difficult to hear.

Caleb might have found Noah's comments amusing if they hadn't reminded him of Aunt Eleanor's insistence that a mail-order bride was a foolish venture. The morning was turning into a family feud rather than the neighbor variety. It struck Caleb that he'd better head home before a fistfight broke out after all.

Caleb turned his horse. "Good day, gentlemen. I'll send my men to repair the fence if you're agreeable."

"Aw, heck, I don't care about the fence," Seth grumbled. "Do whatever you please. I'll be happy to pay my part if you send me a bill."

As he rode back to the ranch house, Caleb noted the men's amused responses. They spoke amongst themselves, trying to keep their voices low so Caleb wouldn't hear, but he heard anyway. William remarked that the mail-order brides were already a success, considering they'd helped forge a truce between Seth Bailey and Caleb Walker.

Caleb might have smiled at the exchange between Seth and Noah. Any other time he would have found Noah's words amusing, especially since he joked at the expense of his brother. Instead, he revisited Noah's words with a heavy heart.

*That ain't what's getting off the boat.*

Noah's words sparked small shards of worry inside Caleb's heart, for Noah spoke of the woman who would care for a small, defenseless baby. A child who had already lost so much.

# Chapter Seven

**Abigail**

Abigail and Laura worked on the cabin, sweeping and cleaning until the room smelled fresh and appealing. Even though it was clean, Abigail still didn't especially wish to sleep there. She'd found evidence of rats, which touched on some of her deepest childhood fears.

Despite her worry, she wore a cheerful smile, chatted with Laura and even tried to make little Francine smile.

To pass the time, the two women chatted about their lives in Boston. Abigail told Laura about Miss Peabody's shameful jilting and how her groom had surprised them on deck that afternoon. Laura expressed dismay. She could scarcely believe any man could stoop so low as to leave his poor bride at the altar.

Laura proved to be a charming companion. Despite her elegant dress, she applied herself to the task of cleaning the room. She seemed especially concerned for the sake of her small charge, murmuring fretful comments about the child taking a chill from the dank air in the lower compartments.

The commotion aboveboard told the girls the crew was about to set sail. They finished their work and ascended the narrow, rickety staircase.

"I should check on Miss Peabody," Abigail said, pausing at the top of the lower stairs. "It will only take a moment."

Laura shook her head. "I'll go along. The poor dear might need some assistance."

"She always needs something," Abigail said. She went on in a hushed, apologetic tone. "I don't mean to complain, but I'm still somewhat taken aback that she agreed to come on such a voyage to begin with. She's not the hardiest sort of women."

"Maybe the journey will do her good. Everyone can use a fresh start at some point in their life. A clean slate and whatnot."

Abigail gave her a grateful smile. They made their way down the hallway of the first-class passengers. The aisle was a sight different than the steerage compartments below. The hall was wide, lined with a bright, woolen tapestry runner with cheerful lanterns lighting the way. The gas lights flickered, casting a warm glow across the burnished wood wall panels.

They paused at Miss Peabody's door. Abigail knocked softly and waited. She debated simply opening the door and entering but didn't want to disturb Miss Peabody if she was resting. She knocked once more, to no avail.

"She's probably exhausted," Laura said. "She suffered quite a shock with that dastardly fiancé arriving just as she boarded the ship."

"I won't be at ease until I see her and know she is well," Abigail fretted.

"The poor dear has suffered too much excitement. Some ladies can't tolerate that much strain."

Abigail glanced wistfully at the door. "I suppose I should let her rest. I can bring her a supper later this evening. Perhaps she'll have recovered by then."

Shouting overhead drew their attention. Laura's eyes lit with excitement. "It's time to set sail. Let's go to the railing and wave."

"Wave? To whom? Do you have someone there to see you off?"

Laura shook her head. "I don't have anybody sending me off, but it sounds like the thing to do. Come on! It will be fun! When will we see Boston again?"

Abigail wanted to tell her she'd be back in a few months' time but thought better of it. She didn't want to explain her situation to Laura. Not just yet. What if the girl were to mention the news to Miss Peabody? It would hurt Miss Peabody's feelings immensely. She'd view Abigail's plans as a betrayal.

Abigail gave the woman's firmly closed door one final look and nodded. "All right. Let's see what all the fuss is about."

They went upstairs and each girl took little Francine by the hand as they strolled the deck, seeking a place at the railing. Laura fussed and fretted when the child tried to wrest her hand free. She confided to Abigail she worried about the child falling overboard.

"It was my greatest fear when I made my plans to take her along," Laura said. "But I couldn't possibly leave her behind."

Abigail marveled that Laura had the courage to bring a child on an ocean voyage. Not only for fear of the water, but for fear of what her husband-to-be might say. Clearly, he didn't expect his bride to arrive with a child in tow. Laura had explained that he'd sent money for a small room in first-class but she had exchanged the room so she could buy passage for the girl.

"You wouldn't know it, but this little darling used to be quite the chatterbox," Laura said. "Her mother brought her to the shop when she was just a baby. We all adored her. She grew to be a lively child and actually spoke in full sentences by the time she was two."

Francine averted her gaze. Abigail felt sorry for her. She could tell the girl didn't want to be the subject of any conversation.

"Oh, go on, you," Laura said gently, stroking the back of her hand against the child's cheek. "You're quiet as a mouse now, but one of your first words was *my* name."

Francine's lips twitched with a hint of a smile.

"That's quite an honor," Abigail marveled. "I can't imagine how that must feel to be so important to a little one."

"Francine, darling, did you hear?" Laura asked. "Maybe by the time we reach Texas, you'll call Abigail by name."

Francine looked up shyly, regarding Abigail from beneath a fringe of long, dark lashes. Abigail's breath caught in her throat. Something in the girl's fragile look made Abigail's heart squeeze. In that instant, she understood why Laura had brought the child along. How could she leave such a precious and vulnerable little one behind?

They found a spot near the railing to watch the crew cast off the moorings. The crowd's excitement grew. Shouts filled the air along with well wishes.

"You don't see Mr. Penobscot in the crowd, do you?" Laura asked. Her mouth curved with a teasing smile. "Or perhaps he's hidden himself on board as a stowaway."

"Hush, you," Abigail chided, hardly able to keep from laughing. "I'm sure I've seen the last of him."

Abigail wished Miss Peabody had come above board to see the fanfare. She was missing out on all the fun, probably snoring through the entire departure.

The crew tossed the ropes to the pier one by one. When the final one dropped to the wet planks, the passengers let out a cheer as did the spectators. A band played a jaunty tune. Women waved handkerchiefs. Men shouted bon voyage.

Free of the moorings, the ship moved away from the pier and slowly made its way through the harbor. As the ship gained momentum, the prow plowed through the waves. The sails snapped and billowed as the wind filled the broad swathes of canvas. The ship skimmed the waves, sending a spray across the shimmering surface. Curving in a graceful arc, the ship headed out of the harbor, setting a course for the open water.

Abigail's heart pounded against her ribs.

In the last few weeks, she'd been so busy running hither and yon, helping Miss Peabody prepare for the journey, she hadn't imagined the voyage itself.

And yet here they were, leaving Boston.

They stayed at the railing and watched the harbor fade in the distance. The sun set. The evening stars appeared one by one in the violet skies. Abigail was so overcome she could hardly find the words to say as much. From the look on Laura's face, her new friend felt the same.

As the last rays of sunlight faded, the dinner bell rang. The girls went downstairs to the second-class dining hall, where they dined on a simple dinner of boiled ham, stewed spinach and boiled potatoes. The food was quite good, a fact which came as a surprise.

After the meal, Abigail went upstairs and requested a tray from the first-class dining room. While she waited, she peeked around the corner to steal a glimpse of the fancy salon. Passengers dressed in all their finery sipped champagne and nibbled elegant foods. No boiled ham in first class, Abigail noted.

A quartet played in the far corner. Violin notes hung in the air. Nothing like the music that played below. Abigail cringed as she recalled the bawdy songs the steerage passengers sang when their meal was done. She hoped that little Francine would have no memory of the songs or antics below.

One of the waitstaff brought the tray. She met Francine and Laura outside and the three of them traipsed to Miss Peabody's cabin.

The hallways were quiet. The first-class passengers would likely remain in the dining rooms and smoking rooms until late into the evening. Her heart squeezed with dismay just as it had earlier. She wished that Miss Peabody would leave her room. There was so much to see and enjoy.

When they arrived at Miss Peabody's room, Laura knocked on the door as Abigail had her hands full, holding the tray. Again, there was no answer. Laura knocked a little louder this time. Abigail called Miss Peabody's name.

Nothing.

A slow sense of alarm crept over Abigail. She tried to push her worries aside but could not. Wordlessly, she gave the tray to Laura. The time for decorum had passed. She turned the handle and pushed the door. It swung open easily enough to reveal an empty room.

Abigail stepped inside. "Miss Peabody?"

Laura followed her with little Francine at her heels. She set the tray down on a table in the center of the room.

Abigail called the name of her mistress again, this time with a note of urgency. Her voice trembled. She rushed to the bedroom alcove and found it empty. Laura came behind her and with a shaking hand pointed at the note left on the pillow.

It was Miss Peabody's writing, to be sure, but it was clear she'd written the note in a hurry. The note had only a few hasty lines. Abigail shook her head with profound bewilderment. The letter didn't make sense. Nothing made sense. Her thoughts spun with confusion and a growing sense of dread. She read the lines again, this time aloud, her voice no more than a trembling whisper.

*Abigail, I must inform you that I've changed my mind regarding my Texas venture. My darling Reginald returned. He explained that he had written to postpone the wedding, but the note was lost. Can you imagine? He made one last, desperate plea, begging me to stay in Boston. I was set to refuse him. I still felt very cross with him for the mortification he caused me, but he fell to his knees and swore to throw himself from the ship if I didn't forgive him. There was no time to find you or retrieve my trunks.*

*Regards,*

*Harriet Peabody*

# Chapter Eight

**Caleb**

Over the course of the next week, his aunt hardly left Caleb's side. From the moment she woke till the moment she retired for the day, she followed close behind. The only time he got a moment's peace was when he went to the barn or out with his men to work in the pastures.

She confessed her fear that the instant she turned her back, he'd run off and marry "some poor, dejected spinster bride." Somehow Eleanor had surmised that Miss Peabody was older than he was. To her thinking, that confirmed the notion that the woman was a spinster.

Having her at the house had been a trial. It had, however, allowed him to travel a little more freely. With his aunt in his home, he could leave the baby in her care while he traveled to an army camp a day's ride from Sweet Willow. He intended to speak to the commanding officer about the sale of beef for the troops, a transaction that would be at least five thousand head of cattle.

In the past, Caleb had traveled all the time, but he'd scarcely left his ranch since his brother died. The ride to the army camp on the Salado River refreshed his spirits somehow. The fine spring weather made for a pleasant journey.

He arrived just before lunch and took the midday meal with General Fitzhugh and several of his subordinates. The meal was set out in a tent overlooking the river. Caleb was not the only guest. There were two other ranchers from West Texas present. They all came to bid on the military order of beef.

Caleb gave the two men a polite nod and the group chatted amiably about cattle drives, recent floods and the prospect of the railroads building a line north.

Although the men passed a pleasant afternoon, Caleb had the distinct feeling that the general only wanted to give the appearance of interest in the other men's business. Caleb couldn't help feeling a small glimmer of pride.

In the past, he and his men had delivered up to ten thousand head to various Army outposts. From there, the military took command of the animals and partitioned the herd to various camps across the South.

The general, a tall, wiry man, had the energy of a man half his age. Charles Fitzhugh had served his entire life in the military. Despite his long deployments to various outposts, the man was a devoted family man. He often spoke fondly of his numerous children. He claimed he intended to retire soon as his eldest daughter had married and expected his first grandchild.

After coffee was served, General Fitzhugh bid the other ranchers a good day, thanking them for making the trip to Salado. Both men looked taken aback at the dismissal. Both gave Caleb a stern look as if he'd somehow wrangled a deal out from under them. Caleb ignored the glares. He sighed a breath of satisfaction as the commanding officer saw the men off.

Raising and selling cattle - that's what he was meant to do. Running a household, especially one with a small child - that was a different matter. His thoughts drifted to Justin.

Before Caleb had left that morning at dawn, he'd paused at the boy's door as he often did. He remained until he heard the child's light breathing. As soon as he knew the boy slept peacefully, he left the house.

Without thinking, his hand moved to his breast pocket. While the general remained outside seeing the other men off, Caleb tugged the letter from his pocket. How many times had he read the letter? A hundred times?

Aunt Eleanor would sneer at his feelings for a woman he'd never met. Especially if she ever saw him rereading the letters. He ran his fingers over the tidy writing and read the poem inscribed at the bottom of the page.

Maybe he was getting tender-hearted. He hated to think that was the case. A man in his position needed to stay vigilant and keep his heart tightly locked. Thoughts of romance had no place in the wilds of Texas. Particularly since he'd promised his bride a marriage of convenience.

The general returned, surprising Caleb, drawing him from his thoughts.

"You know I have to let other ranchers bid on the cattle purchase," he said, a grin tipping his lips. "Three quotes. Impartial. You know the drill."

"Yes sir. I understand," Caleb replied.

"The military only cares about what it's going to cost them. They're less concerned if the animals arrive on time or are half-starved from the trip."

Caleb gave him an answering smile. "Yes, sir, you know that I'll honor any agreement on price as well as delivery date."

The general sat down across the table. He leaned back in his chair and regarded Caleb with a thoughtful look. "An army marches on its stomach. I'm not moving my men anytime soon. Just the same, soldiers appreciate good vittles. If the cooks serve them a plate of tough gristle one night, the malcontents start acting up. If that happens *every* night, even my best men are likely to gripe and shirk."

"I understand. I like to give my men and the herd plenty of time to make the trip. It's important that the animals graze and rest. Otherwise, they're nothing more than skin and bones when they arrive."

The general scoffed. "And that's *if* they arrive. General Barton up in Kansas wrote me last month. He told me his order of cattle never arrived last winter. His men ate beans for Christmas while snow piled up shoulder high."

Caleb rubbed his chin. "Maybe I ought to send General Barton a friendly letter, offering my services."

General Fitzhugh laughed and shook his head. "You're a man of business. I like that about you. And you're a man of your word. I like that even better."

The man's gaze drifted to the table where Caleb had inadvertently left Miss Peabody's letter. His brow lifted with interest, seeming to note the feminine script.

Caleb took the letter, returning it to his pocket. He didn't care for anyone to see the writing. The words were for him alone. He wanted to keep them close to his heart far from prying eyes.

"A letter from a sweetheart?" General Fitzhugh asked.

"It is, in fact. My intended."

"Excellent. A woman is always a civilizing influence on the world of men. I've been married over twenty years and I still count the days until I see my Gwendoline."

Caleb offered a polite smile. He was at a loss as to what to say about that. Civilizing influence? He supposed that might be true. What struck him even more was the notion of having tender feelings for a wife of twenty years. It seemed astonishing. Hard to imagine. Despite his disbelief, he felt a pang of longing, even a little envy.

The general's eyes misted. He coughed and growled, taking a swallow of his coffee to compose himself. Caleb's jaw dropped a notch. The tough, battle-hardened general seemed momentarily overcome by thoughts of his wife.

"I wish you the best," General Fitzhugh said gruffly. "Women in these parts are as rare as hen's teeth."

Caleb nodded. He didn't care to explain that his intended came all the way from Boston. He was certain the old military man would embark on some unflattering remarks about northerners.

The man steepled his fingers and continued. "I certainly never imagined married life. I never fathomed the way a wife can be such a comfort to a man."

The general gazed past the door, his eyes losing their focus as a nostalgic smile played upon his lips. Caleb dismissed the man's words. Leaving the ranch and tending to business had helped him clear his mind. Here amongst men, he was able to reaffirm his priorities. Ranching. Building something worthwhile to leave his nephew.

Caleb was pleased to receive a wife, to be sure. He'd spent more time than he cared to admit in the anticipation of his betrothed. Still, he understood full well that marriage was nothing more than a practical matter despite the pretty words that adorned the letters from his bride.

When he left the camp a short time later, he had a contract for delivery of five thousand head at the price he'd asked. The cattle drive wouldn't take more than two days. He would send the cattle with William when the time came because by then he would have a wife and would start his new life as a family man.

# Chapter Nine

**Abigail**

Abigail couldn't have realized how much she would treasure Laura's kindness and steadfastness during her first night aboard *The Sparrow*. Abigail almost fainted after reading Miss Peabody's note.

Laura sprang into action, fussing and waiting upon Abigail, insisting she rest. She asked the ship's crew if they'd seen Miss Peabody, but no one had. Laura inquired in the dining room as well, searched the decks for a woman fitting the description Abigail gave her.

When it became clear that Miss Peabody had truly stayed behind in Boston, Laura suggested Abigail move out of steerage and into the better rooms.

"You deserve to stay in her rooms. She's mistreated you terribly. Besides, the room is simply going to sit empty. Why not?"

Abigail was taken aback. The idea shocked her almost as much as Miss Peabody leaving her behind. She looked around the cabin, taking in the luxury and refinement of the spacious rooms. Unlike her cabin below, Miss Peabody's quarters had many windows.

Outside the ship lay a blanket of darkness. Faint light came from the half-moon peeping above the horizon. The night sky stretched as far as she could see. Stars twinkled over the broad expanse of waves. It was beautiful and yet the sight filled her with loneliness, adding to her dread.

"Would you and Francine stay with me?" she asked.

Laura thought for a moment. "I suppose we could."

Cabin number sixteen had a large, spacious bedroom with a four-poster bed. A washroom, complete with a tub and sink. The sitting room had a day bed and chaise. After some deliberation, they decided upon a sleeping arrangement. Laura insisted that Abigail take the large bed. She and Francine would bed down in the sitting room.

Two ship maids came to prepare the room for evening. They brought extra blankets and pillows. Abigail felt like a fraud as the maids, girls her own age, tended to the beds, turning down the covers and plumping the pillows. When they left, she let out a sigh of relief.

If it hadn't been for Laura's stalwart support, Abigail might have collapsed into a sobbing heap. Never had she felt so terrified. Laura encouraged her, however. Over the course of the evening, they unpacked their meager belongings. Anytime Abigail felt a wave of self-pity, little Francine was the one to coax a smile from her.

The girl delighted in the sea travel. She was drawn to the windows, seemingly enchanted by the moonlight on the water. Gazing at the sea, the girl wore a slight smile and even hummed every so often.

"I feel I should point something out," Laura said a few hours after they set sail. "And that is you should not feel a shred of guilt for using the rooms." She spoke as she riffled through Miss Peabody's trunks. "I would not mind staying in the sheep barn downstairs. I'm not one to fuss, but I worry about Francine. She's been through so much. And you, my dear, have suffered quite a shock. I, for one, am grateful for such a lovely room."

Abigail sat on the edge of her bed and sipped her tea, musing that, on this ship, she was no longer a servant. The tea had been brought *to her* by the first-class valet, the first time someone had *served her*. She also liked Laura's use of the phrase *"sheep barn."*

"Miss Peabody must have been somewhat stout." Laura held up one of Miss Peabody's new dresses. "I think I can make the necessary adjustments."

Abigail set her cup on the bedside table. "What sort of adjustments?"

"I'm going to take in the bodice a few inches so it will fit you, of course." She made a face. "You can't go to the first-class dining hall in a muslin frock. Remember, you're Miss Peabody, as far as the crew are concerned."

Abigail blinked. "Well, I suppose I am, or I could manage that sort of charade. If not, the room would be empty, and we'd be in the dank quarters below. Still, the gowns don't belong to me. I wouldn't feel right taking Miss Peabody's fine things."

She glanced down at her plain dress.

Laura didn't bother with a reply. She rummaged in her own trunk for a measuring tape. Humming as she arranged her things the way she liked them, she called Francine for a hand and gave her a box of pins. The little girl needed no instruction. She stood patiently and somber as a sentry, holding the pins for Laura.

Abigail hung back, reluctant to put on the fine gown Laura held up for her.

"Come then, Abigail," Laura fussed. "I'll need to measure your waist and bosom. With any luck, I won't need to hem the skirt. Was your mistress much taller than you?"

"No," Abigail replied, crossing the cabin. "We were about the same height."

"Ah, thank goodness for small favors. This won't take long at all."

Abigail swallowed hard. A pang of guilt pained her conscience. She let Laura fit her for the pretty dress. She then readied for bed, said her prayers and sank into the immense bed. Shivering beneath the blankets, she tried not to listen to Laura tearing the seams from Miss Peabody's dress.

Later that night, she tossed and turned, feeling lost in the massive four-poster bed. One moment, she fumed that Miss Peabody had left her behind. The next moment, she fretted that her mistress might be mistreated once more by Mr. Penobscot.

In the furthest reaches of her mind, Abigail agonized over what might happen when she arrived in Texas. How would she explain things to Mr. Walker? Would he rail against her? Accuse her of some mischief or wrongdoing? The worst part of all was the prospect of asking the man to loan her money for a ticket back to Boston.

What if he refused? He owed her nothing. There was little to stop him from washing his hands of her the instant she explained her plight.

And then what? She'd have to fend for herself. A stranger in a strange land. Surely, Mr. Walker would help her. She prayed he would take pity on her. How else would she manage?

Miss Peabody had waxed poetic about the man's gallantry. Abigail dared to hope he might treat her gently. A small glimmer of optimism sparked in her heart. Quickly and without an ounce of hesitation, she snuffed the tiny spark of hope. It was best not to hope for anything. She'd learned her lesson well as a child when she waited for her papa and mama to return for her. The years of waiting had been sustained by childish hopes.

Expectation led to crushing disappointment.

She closed her eyes, pulled the blanket tighter and banished any hint of hope from her heart. While she might be forced to travel to Texas, she wouldn't grovel. She wouldn't expect kind treatment from anyone. She'd simply use her wits, try her best to make amends for Miss Peabody's ignoble actions, and ultimately, accept God's plan.

The next morning, Laura had almost finished with the dress. She directed Abigail to stand on the stool. She took her measurements once more, helped her put on the dress and studied the waist and bodice. The lace fabric was more elegant than anything Abigail had ever worn. Laura, however, seemed to think nothing of the material.

She prattled on about the boots Miss Peabody had brought and that they looked as though they might fit. She went on about the other dresses and how long it would take to alter them. Abigail offered a weak protest to which Laura responded with a mischievous chuckle.

While Miss Peabody had left her clothes, Abigail noticed she had taken her candies.

By the time the lunch bell rang, Laura had finished the dress. She'd insisted Abigail wear it along with a fine pair of boots made of leather, soft as a pair of lady's kid gloves. With a few deft movements, Laura swept Abigail's hair into an elegant chignon. Abigail stared at her reflection in the looking glass, hardly able to believe what she saw. She almost didn't recognize herself.

A moment later, Laura led them to the first-class dining room, presiding over the group as if she were the headmistress directing a group of school children. Abigail and Francine followed obediently.

They were seated with two elderly ladies, Emmaline and Coraline. Abigail sat frozen with a burgeoning fear, certain that everyone in the tasteful dining room would know she was an imposter.

Laura chatted with their two companions over the first course of consommé. Both Emmaline and Coraline remarked on the charming girl. By the time the main course arrived, the two ladies seemed to think Laura and Abigail were sisters and that Francine was Laura's daughter.

Abigail tried to respond, but Laura shushed her.

"There's no need to correct everyone, Miss Peabody," Laura said with an impish grin when the two ladies were distracted.

"I feel like a fraud, sitting here amidst all this grandeur. I'm so nervous I can hardly eat a bite."

"Eat your filet," Laura said, eyeing Abigail's full plate. "You could use a little meat on your bones. Men like a lady with some curves."

"What difference does it make what men like?"

Laura batted her lashes and merely laughed.

After lunch, the girls accompanied the two ladies to the deck for an afternoon stroll. Both Coraline and Emmaline wore outlandish hats. Their hats were adorned with plumes and ribbons. Anytime the girls lagged waiting for Francine to catch up, they could easily find the ladies among the other first-class passengers. Their plumage waved merrily in the sea breezes.

At times, the ship seemed to travel close to land. Every so often, they could spy the shore and a hillock would appear along the horizon. The sight of land left Abigail with a surge of homesickness. She'd never imagined leaving Boston for long. Now she couldn't imagine how she might return. With each mile the ship sailed, she drew closer to an uncertain fate.

Secretly, she still held hope that the letters from so long ago were mistaken. She imagined her parents hadn't passed away. She couldn't help a small wistful yearning every so often and she'd wake from dreams of a sister, a fair-haired girl named Sarah.

The thought of a sister only made her feel even more sad. She pushed the notion aside.

When the ship sailed into a storm, she wondered with terror if she might not even reach Texas, much less return to Boston. The ship rocked and pitched. The winds howled across the water, raising waves that crested with white peaks.

The girls retired to their cabin, praying for calmer seas. As the sun set in the dark skies, Laura became ill from the rough passage. She lay in bed, trying not to moan pitifully. Francine grew visibly distressed, which prompted Abigail to sit with the girl and try to comfort her. Laura directed her to a valise which contained books and toys. Abigail and the girl passed the evening reading. Instead of going to the dining room, they requested dinner in the room.

By bedtime, Abigail began to feel queasy. She wore a brave face, however, to keep Francine from growing even more fretful. She helped the girl get into her gown and together they said their prayers. Abigail did the praying, but Francine knelt by her bedside, hands clasped eyes closed. The sight of her in prayer brought a smile to Abigail's face despite the frightful storm.

Abigail prayed for better weather and for Laura to feel better. Silently, she added a prayer for Miss Peabody. She couldn't find it in her heart to resent the woman for too long, even with the ship tossing on the churning seas.

The night passed. Dawn broke with gray and heavy skies, but the seas were markedly calmer. The girls gave thanks for the change in weather. Francine, to their surprise, added a soft "amen."

Feeling revived, Laura set about altering the rest of Miss Peabody's dresses. Abigail tried to convince her that her efforts weren't necessary, but Laura was determined.

"You need a wardrobe more than your mistress," she insisted. "I can't abide by the threadbare frocks you're so fond of. I want to show off your pretty face and graceful figure and I intend to do just that."

"How will I explain any of this to Miss Peabody?"

"You need to put that woman out of your mind."

Over the course of the next few days, Abigail forgot about the pretense of calling herself Miss Peabody. The storm had made so many worries fade from their minds. Even Laura seemed not to care about the prospect of persuading her fiancé to allow Francine to remain with her.

All three girls spent their time on board enjoying the sights and sounds of the voyage. Each night they dined with Emmaline and Coraline. The women wore different, outrageous feathered hats each night, which amused Abigail and Laura to no end. Even Francine grinned at the display.

With little choice, Abigail, Laura and Francine began to enjoy the voyage.

The girls savored the delicious foods, attended concerts and plays and took long walks on the deck. At night, they slept in luxury. The days slipped past. She thought about Mr. Walker's letters every day, and picked them up more than once, but knew that they weren't meant for her. In fact, none of this was meant for her.

Before either of the girls realized it, they neared the Texas shores.

The reality of what awaited them grew visibly in the distance. Standing on the prow, they watched in silence, lost in their thoughts. Land appeared on the horizon as they turned toward Galveston. They had only a few more hours aboard *The Sparrow*. Only Francine acted as if nothing at all was amiss.

# Chapter Ten

**Caleb**

The time had come to go to Galveston to meet his intended. The weather had turned, however, with cold, bitter downpours, and a flurry of illnesses and complaints. Caleb intended to take the baby with him to Galveston to greet his bride. With the wet roads nearly impassable, he considered going alone and leaving the baby in his aunt's care.

Eleanor had resigned herself to Caleb's scheme for a mail order bride, but dearly wished to go with him to meet her. To her delight, the day before he was to depart, the rainclouds cleared, leaving lush green lands in their wake.

Caleb bundled up the child as well as Aunt Eleanor and made the three-hour journey to the port of Galveston. The group set out the day before the ship was to arrive, traveling by buggy. Caleb had ordered three rooms at the Driscoll Hotel, the finest hotel in the area, one he hoped would meet his aunt's approval and that of Miss Peabody as well.

The notion that he was soon to meet his intended put him in an uneasy mood. It didn't help matters that his aunt made comments about his bride, small biting remarks that galled him. The baby, thankfully, slumbered in his bassinet in the back of the buggy. As they approached Galveston, his aunt grew quieter. Still, just to make her disapproval perfectly clear, she rode with her nose in the air.

Caleb was grateful for a reprieve from her words. They checked into the rooms. He managed to feed the baby, not bothering to order a hot bath for the bottle. Sad to say, it wasn't Justin's first cold bottle. Caleb had, in desperation, fed the child cold milk in the past whenever the boy hollered loudly enough.

He spent a restless night, filled with doubts and absurd imaginings of meeting his bride. The next morning dawned with clear skies and mild weather. This boded well, he decided. At least it would mean that his aunt and nephew would be able to come with him to the harbor. He didn't relish the notion of introducing his aunt to his intended, but that would have to happen eventually.

He ordered the horses to be hitched to the buggy. After he helped his aunt to the seat and gave her the dozing child to hold, they set off on the short trip to the Galveston pier. By the time they arrived, they could spy the ship's sails on the horizon.

The crowd gathered on the pier. Somewhere amidst the throng waited Caleb's neighbor. Seth Bailey was out there, awaiting his bride but without a child in his care. Caleb scanned the mass of people but didn't see Bailey anywhere.

The ship drew closer. The crew prepared to receive the vessel, hurrying up and down the pier, hauling ropes and luggage wagons. The crowd pushed against the barriers, eager to meet their loved ones. Caleb hung back, unwilling to wade amidst the bustling crowd with his elderly aunt and nephew.

The ship docked. The gangplank lowered. The first-class passengers gathered on the railing, waving to the crowd below. Among the first passengers were two aged ladies wearing plumed hats. Somehow, despite their feeble appearance, they managed a favorable position amongst the passengers and led the disembarking group.

"Ah, there's Miss Peabody now," Aunt Eleanor remarked drily. "And look, the poor dear has brought along a friend. How very lovely. I must say she has delightful taste in hats."

Caleb frowned at his aunt. He was too nervous to appreciate her wit. "Miss Peabody is traveling alone, I'll have you know. She wanted to bring her maid but I wouldn't allow it."

His aunt's lips quirked. "Why, Caleb. That wasn't very civil of you."

"I didn't want a girl tagging along."

He didn't add that his mandate had served as a sort of test. He wanted a wife of convenience, but he also wanted a wife who would conveniently do his bidding. If she had insisted on having her way, he would have seen her refusal as obstinance.

He also wouldn't mention that he had a few other tests for the woman before he'd agree to marry her. What he intended to find out was how well she managed the baby's care. He didn't need a beautiful wife. He didn't need a doting wife. He needed a tender-hearted wife who would care for Justin as if he were her own.

The baby fussed in his arms. Aunt Eleanor gave the child a sympathetic look, set her cane in the crook of her arm, and took the child from him. He patted the boy's shoulder affectionately as the child settled in her embrace. Eleanor sighed happily, closing her eyes with happiness.

A cry pierced the air, followed by a shriek. Caleb thought his mind might be playing tricks on him. None of the crowd responded. Not even Eleanor seemed to have heard the plaintive cries. He scanned the railing above. Most of the passengers milled about the gate to the gangplank, but two women stood near the prow, both in clear distress, gazing at the water below.

"Francine," came an anguished cry from one of the women.

Caleb watched in astonished dismay as the other woman clambered over the railing and plunged to the water. He shook his head and with a growl, pushed his way through the throng.

"Eh, watch it," came the words of a bystander. "The nerve!" came the response from a pair of women. Others grumbled and tried to block his path. Behind him, he heard his aunt call his name. He ignored them all, his attention fixed on a spot in the water where the girl splashed and flailed and then disappeared beneath the murky depths.

Caleb reached the edge of the pier. Without hesitation, he jumped into the water. The cold drew a snarl from his chest. He reached the flailing girl. She struggled to keep her head above the water, not because of her sodden dress, although that couldn't have helped matters, but because she held a small child in her arms. The child, a small girl, flailed and cried with terror.

"Take the child," the young woman demanded. A wave splashed over her head, making her cough and sputter. She managed to keep the child's head above the water.

Caleb reached for her.

She gasped for breath, managing a feeble plea. "Take the child!"

"I'll take you both," Caleb growled.

The woman tried to protest, but he would have none of it. He wrapped an arm around her and the child and swam the short distance to the pier. By that time, the commotion had captured the attention of the people on the pier.

Men rushed to help them. Women cried out in dismay. Children wept.

"Take the woman," he commanded the onlookers.

The men pulled the young woman and child onto the pier. Several other men offered to help him. He waved off their assistance.

He staggered to his feet. "Are you all right, miss?" he asked.

She shivered. "Fine, thank you."

The child wept in her arms.

Aunt Eleanor stood on the pier, regarding him with an arched brow. "Of all the events that might unfold this morning, I certainly didn't expect this."

The young woman's companion hurried down the pier. She swept the small child into her arms with a cry of relief.

"I'm not certain if you're the bravest young woman I've met, or the foolhardiest," Aunt Eleanor said to the young woman he'd pulled from the water.

The girl lay in a heap, too weak to protest. Caleb couldn't help feeling more sympathy for the girl. He wanted to shield her from the idle gaze of the spectators and from his aunt's sharp tongue.

The second young woman appeared to feel the same protective notion. She lifted her chin and responded with, "Abigail is very, very brave. She's not foolhardy."

Caleb narrowed his eyes. A slow prickle of awareness moved across his mind. "Your name is Abigail?"

The girl nodded and closed her eyes. She rubbed her forehead, pushing her sodden locks out of her eyes. She was too weak to reply or even meet his gaze.

He crouched beside her. "Did you come with a *Miss Peabody*?"

"Miss Peabody was detained in Boston," the girl said. She blinked as if trying to keep tears from falling.

"Perhaps I should introduce myself," Caleb said, his tone careful and deliberate. "Seeing as we've already become somewhat acquainted."

The girl peered at him with growing consternation.

Caleb tried not to glare at her. What had been a prickle of discomfort a moment before grew to a rush of indignation. Part of his mind refused to believe this young woman could be Miss Peabody's Abigail. Another part of his mind knew that, without a doubt, she was indeed the very same young woman.

"My name is Caleb Walker."

What little color tinged the young woman's cheeks faded away, leaving her as pale as new milk. Instead of replying in kind, she managed a delicate, trembling whisper. "Mr. Walker..."

"That's right."

"I thought you'd be old. And heavyset. Possibly b-bald."

He wasn't sure what to say to that. Why would she assume those things? He wasn't any of those things and liked to think he was passably handsome. Ladies often said he was easy on the eyes and some small, vain part of him assumed they were right. He felt a little affronted that this lovely young woman seemed to assume he'd be ugly.

He should be mad about Miss Peabody. Instead, he was mad this wisp of a girl insulted his looks.

It didn't help that the longer he looked at her, the prettier she seemed. Despite her bedraggled appearance, she stole his breath.

He heard the unmistakable sound of his aunt's chuckle somewhere behind him. Eleanor probably was enjoying this.

Seth Bailey, if he was watching, would laugh all the way back to Sweet Willow.

What a turn of events. How had this happened? After all the care he'd taken finding a matchmaking agency, he'd been duped.

# Chapter Eleven

**Abigail**

One moment, she'd walked the railing with Laura and Francine, preparing to disembark the ship. The next, Laura had left her side to chase after Francine's bonnet. The wind had taken it from the child's hand and whisked it away. Francine became frantic and had clambered atop a crate, trying to catch a glimpse of Laura. And in the next moment, the child had tumbled off the ship.

A half hour later, Abigail sat on the pier, shivering in her sodden dress, waiting for her trunks. Laura and Francine had left with Mr. Bailey. Abigail had been so shaken from the mishap that she hardly remembered their hasty goodbye.

Mr. Walker collected her trunks and came to collect her too.

"I suppose you're my responsibility for the time being," he remarked gruffly.

Abigail was too cold to give a coherent reply. He frowned, took off his jacket and wrapped it around her shoulders. After a short buggy ride, they arrived at their hotel. Abigail changed out of her dress, washed hurriedly and put on a new dress.

The frock had a long, basque bodice trimmed with velvet. Buttons decorated the sides of the narrow skirt. Laura said the pale blue complimented her eyes. Abigail found herself wondering what Mr. Walker would think.

He was nothing like what she'd imagined. He was head and shoulders taller than her. Powerfully built. Unsmiling. She cringed at her suggestion he would be stout and fat. What must he have thought?

He sent a porter to her room with a note about dining together. The note came across as a command rather than an invitation.

His friendliness didn't improve over the course of dinner. They sat in the dining room of the hotel. He glowered across the table. His aunt sat between them, a smile playing upon her lips. The baby rested in the room upstairs, tended by a hotel nursemaid.

"That Miss Peabody had lovely taste in frocks," his aunt remarked.

"Thank you, Mrs. Walker."

"Call me Eleanor."

Abigail nodded and, unable to resist, stole a quick glance at Mr. Walker, wondering if he might tell her to call him by his given name. His cold expression made it clear he had no use for such niceties.

Abigail tugged her woolen shawl closer around her shoulders. She still felt a chill from the icy waters despite the warmth of a nearby blaze burning in a fireplace.

"I intend to return her belongings to her," Abigail said. "It's just a matter of acquiring a ticket back to Boston."

"You think I'll pay for passage back?" Mr. Walker asked.

"I can reimburse you," Abigail replied. "I work. I have a little money tucked away, money that Mr. and Mrs. Peabody left me. I've left my account in Miss Peabody's care."

It was a fact. Miss Peabody's parents had given Abigail a small sum of money in return for staying on to care for their daughter. Abigail hadn't a clue as to how much money was in the account, but she'd already resolved to pay Mr. Walker for any expenses she cost him.

Mr. Walker gave her a skeptical look. Abigail had to admit they hadn't gotten off to the best start, but he'd seemed to grow more vexed with her as the day wore on. The man was nothing like what she expected.

She recalled the strength in his arms as he helped her from the water.

Her face warmed with embarrassment. She tried to keep her mind fixed upon the unmistakable fact that Mr. Walker was a surly, unpleasant man, one given to dark, accusing looks.

The only time he didn't have a disagreeable countenance was when he mentioned the baby. It was then that she glimpsed a softer, more tender side to the man. They ate dinner, mostly in silence, the only small talk came from Eleanor.

"I have a proposal that might suit you," Eleanor said when the waiter served coffee and sherbet.

Abigail set the dish of sherbet aside. The thought of eating a cold dessert didn't appeal to her, not with the chill she still felt deep in her bones.

Eleanor went on. "You could stay with my nephew and great-nephew until the next ship sets sail for Boston and I'll pay your way back."

Abigail shivered. She didn't need to look at Mr. Walker to know he would regard the proposal with a scowl.

"I cannot accept your kind offer," Abigail said. "It wouldn't do for an unmarried woman to stay with a bachelor. If Miss Peabody were to discover what I'd done, my reputation would be ruined. I'd never find another position in Boston."

Before Eleanor could reply, Mr. Walker spoke. He leaned forward, folding his hands on the table. "You seem to be fond of poetry."

Abigail blinked with surprise. Years ago, Mrs. Peabody had hired a tutor for her. She'd written poetry then. It had been a long time, however. So long she'd almost forgotten.

Mr. Walker went on. "I noticed you write poems. I saw them in the book that fell from your trunks."

"You read my poems?"

"A few."

Her heart raced. She wanted to tell him that he had no right to read the poems she'd written as a young, foolish girl. She flushed with embarrassment.

"Are they yours?"

"I don't need to answer that."

"Or did you steal them from Harriet Peabody, just like your dresses and passage to Galveston?"

Abigail shrank back, stunned by the accusation.

"Caleb," Eleanor said firmly. "Don't speak to the poor girl like that. What could you be thinking?"

Mr. Walker kept his eyes fixed on her. He tugged a letter from his pocket and slid it across the table. Her hands trembling, Abigail took the letter and read Miss Peabody's words. The correspondence held nothing out of the ordinary, just a few details about life in Boston.

The words were familiar because she had come up with them while Miss Peabody wrote them down. It was only when Abigail reached the end that she understood the cause of Mr. Walker's fury. For there, at the close of the letter, Miss Peabody had written a poem. The words were a direct copy of one of Abigail's poems, poems she never discussed with anybody.

"I've never shown my poems to anyone," she said softly.

Eleanor took the letter from her and after reading it drew a sharp breath. "My word."

Abigail swallowed hard, trying to summon what remained of her courage. "I admit I helped Miss Peabody write her letters. I meant no harm. I only wished to help her. I never imagined she took my poems. I would never have let her use something so dear to my heart. Something I'd written when I was just a girl."

Eleanor folded the letter and tucked it back into the envelope. "Are you quite certain you wish to return to Boston, my dear? Because I can assure you, anyone willing to steal your poetry wouldn't hesitate to take your money."

"I'm sure she wouldn't do such a thing," Abigail argued.

Eleanor simply arched a brow, clearly skeptical.

Abigail didn't know what to say. It was all too much. Too overwhelming. She wasn't a girl given to weeping. She was far too practical, but suddenly she thought she might simply fall apart.

"I'd like to have a word with the girl," Eleanor said to Caleb.

He looked affronted, but without a word of protest left the two women.

"I have to return to Boston," Abigail said. "Not just because of Miss Peabody."

"Why else? Is someone waiting for you there? Someone other than Miss Peabody?"

"No," Abigail said, her eyes stinging again.

Abigail wanted to explain the dreams she had about a sister she might never have met. Her parents might have had another child. It was possible. She clung to the idea. The people at the orphanage told her of another girl but did they really know?

She kept her thoughts to herself. Eleanor didn't seem the type of woman who put stock into silly notions like sisters that appeared in dreams. She was a practical woman. Abigail liked to think the same of herself.

Eleanor folded her hands on the table. "My nephew knows a great deal about ranching. There isn't anything he doesn't know about horses, cattle and land. He's made his fortune entirely on his own. He started with nothing. I refused to encourage his notions and gave him not a penny. Despite that, he's done exceedingly well."

Abigail felt forlorn and defeated, wishing she could be anywhere other than a fancy dining room filled with rich, arrogant strangers. She couldn't understand why Eleanor was talking about Mr. Walker's success.

"My nephew can do many things well. Andrew, my other nephew, could too." She got a faraway look in her eyes. "Andrew... how I miss him. He was the opposite of his twin brother. Quiet. Thoughtful. Bookish. He'd started his work as a medical doctor. But the good Lord had other plans for him."

"I'm sorry," Abigail said. "I truly am."

"If Andrew were here, he could have spoken on Caleb's behalf. Caleb was a rough and tumble boy, full of mischief. Andrew always had a kind word for anyone. He could have explained his gruff brother's ways better than I can."

"You don't need to explain."

"But I do. Because we need you, Abigail. I need you. Caleb does and Justin most of all. I'm asking you to stay on. At least for a short while. *The Sparrow* won't be back to Galveston for a month and a half and heaven knows when other ships shall be along. Stay. Please. If you still wish to return when the ship docks, I'll pay your passage back myself."

Abigail swallowed hard, trying to think of a response.

"Just consider my offer," Eleanor said. "Just think about it."

The weight on her shoulders felt oppressive. She wanted only to close her eyes and wake up in her small, narrow room in the Peabody home. Eleanor hadn't made mention of her limited options. She hadn't pointed out that Abigail had no money, no place to go, and no way to get home. Instead, the woman sat across the table from her waiting, her eyes lit with a kindly light.

"All right," Abigail whispered. "I'll think about it. Thank you."

Eleanor smiled. "Thank *you*, my dear girl."

# Chapter Twelve

**Caleb**

After dinner, they retired to their rooms, with Abigail shutting herself behind the door of the suite adjoining his. Eleanor followed him with the pretense of assuring herself the hotel nursemaid had done an adequate job putting the baby to bed. After she checked the child, she came to his room.

"I've changed my mind," she proclaimed.

"Apparently," Caleb retorted. He stood by the window, his back to her as he took in the sights of Galveston. All day he'd battled with the fury that he'd been duped. Even worse, the young woman who had come in Miss Peabody's stead galled him to no end. He couldn't stop the unwelcome thoughts that pestered his usual well-ordered thinking.

Eleanor's movements behind him told him that she had no intention of leaving him in peace. She'd come to discuss matters. He knew exactly what that meant. A long, drawn-out debate which wouldn't end until his aunt got her way. He should count himself lucky that she wasn't gloating and telling him that she'd told him all along. His plan was foolhardy.

She might yet work that in, however.

He turned to face her. She sat on the chesterfield by the fireplace, a somber look on her face. He was surprised to find no hint of satisfaction in her expression.

A small vial sat on the table before her.

"Do you realize what that contains?" she asked, quietly.

He frowned, crossed the room and picked up the glass bottle. He removed the stopper and sniffed. The contents, a thick, clear oily substance, held an unpleasant scent.

Setting it back on the table, he shrugged. "Something for your leg pain?"

She scoffed. "It *could* be a drug that would alleviate my discomfort. The surgeon suggested such a concoction. I refused, however."

"That doesn't belong to you?"

"It does not. It belongs to the last woman who cared for Justin."

A thread of alarm wound its way through Caleb's mind. Why would a nursemaid carry a bottle of drugs with her? He considered the possibilities, pushing away the more frightening notions.

"She was in pain?"

Eleanor sighed. "No, my dear boy. The bottle contains a sleeping draught."

Caleb shook his head, refusing to believe. Of all the worries that had assailed his mind, fears for the boy's well-being, he hadn't considered a nursemaid might deliberately harm him.

"Go on," he said. "Who did this?"

"Your last girl. Miriam. Or was it Mary? I forget their names. It was the girl with the dark hair. The one who rolled her eyes when she thought you weren't looking."

Caleb winced. He'd hired the last girl from an agency in Houston. She'd come highly recommended and cost him a pretty penny. When Eleanor dismissed the girl, he hadn't bothered to ask why. Eleanor dismissed staff for reasons he didn't always understand. He always attributed her whims to the fact that her standards were higher than his.

He sat down across from her and waited wordlessly. In the room next door, the baby stirred and fretted, but Caleb needed to hear what Eleanor had to say to him. He ignored the baby's soft complaint. A moment passed and the room quieted.

"I discovered the child in his crib at noon," Eleanor said. "His diaper was soiled. He slept so deeply I struggled to wake him. Miriam confessed he hadn't had his morning bottle. I found the vial on the windowsill and dismissed her at once."

Caleb grimaced. His heart thudded heavily in his chest. Leaning forward, he rested his head in his hands. Fear gripped him more tightly than it had since he'd taken the boy into his care. Ranching, cattle, and the world of men he understood. Raising a child seemed fraught with more dangers than any threat he met on the ranch.

Eleanor straightened, narrowing her eyes. "I came to talk you out of a mail-order bride. It seems there isn't one, unless you take into consideration that Miss Peabody used Abigail's words."

"What do you mean by that?"

"You clearly liked what the letters contained. Now you know. The words came from the girl you rescued from the Bay of Galveston."

Caleb's heart lurched inside his chest. He hadn't put two and two together. All that time he'd been rereading the letters, they'd been written by Miss Peabody's maid.

"Abigail threw herself into the water to save a girl she'd only met at the beginning of the voyage. Any woman willing to risk her life for a youngster will do her utmost to care for your son."

*Your son...*

The words sent a jolt down his spine. Eleanor had never said as much before. Anytime she lectured or pontificated on the boy's care, it was always "my nephew".

He nodded. "What do you suggest?"

"Marry this girl."

Caleb snorted. "Really? I know nothing about her. She's not even a Peabody."

Eleanor banged the silver tip of her cane on the floor. Thankfully, it struck the carpet, not the wooden flooring. The last thing he needed was for her to wake Justin.

"Don't you sass your elders, young man," Eleanor retorted. "The two of you would make a fine couple. I'm certain she would never give the child a sleeping draught."

He found himself unable to reply. Over the course of the afternoon, he'd found himself thinking about Abigail constantly. The way her eyes blazed when she looked at him. The way she'd shivered on the pier, her dress dripping, and her hair tumbled past her shoulders. The way she'd felt in his arms when he pulled her from the icy waters.

"I saw the look in your eyes at dinner," Eleanor said.

A smile tugged at her lips. The expression irked Caleb. Eleanor got that look anytime she delivered what she considered to be a splendid idea. It was clear, she thought the whole situation was a perfect solution, as if she'd concocted the entire scheme herself.

"Abigail is no more than a girl," Caleb grumbled.

"I was twelve years younger than Winston."

"She doesn't wish to stay in Texas."

"You will change her mind."

A noise came from the baby's room. The door opened. To Caleb's surprise, Abigail appeared. She held the baby in her arms. Clad in a dressing gown, she fixed her gaze on Eleanor, scarcely acknowledging his presence in the room.

"The baby fussed. Seeing as the caregiver had been dismissed for the evening, I took the liberty of checking on him."

Abigail's gaze drifted to him and her cheeks pinked with embarrassment. He supposed she didn't care to be seen in a dressing gown but hadn't seen the alternative. Her lips pursed with disapproval and he realized he was smiling like a fool. He schooled his features to appear indifferent. Forcing his eyes from the soft disarray of her hair, he noted with even more surprise the way the baby rested in her arms. Instead of squalling, Justin nestled softly in the crook of Abigail's neck.

"Perhaps someone would be so kind as to bring me a bottle," Abigail said, her tone an attempt to recover some shred of lost dignity.

"Certainly," Eleanor replied. "It won't take a moment, my dear girl."

Abigail lifted her chin, patted the boy's back and departed the room.

Eleanor's smile widened as she regarded him with triumph. "Excellent. I won't need to worry about you convincing the girl to stay." She waved a dismissive hand. "As if *you* had any charm."

Caleb opened his mouth to protest her harsh words. He could be charming. No examples of his charm came readily to his mind, but he felt he should argue with the accusation. He searched his memory for a demonstration of his manners and charisma, failing to summon a single instance.

She cut off his reply, silencing him with a stern look and continued. "The baby, thank goodness, will do a great deal of the convincing. I intend to use my powers of persuasion as well."

# Chapter Thirteen

**Abigail**

Abigail did as she promised. She thought about Eleanor's offer all night long. By dawn, she'd decided she couldn't stay. It was impossible.

The Walkers had invited her to breakfast in the dining room, but Abigail refused the invitation. Instead, she wrote a letter to Laura, or rather tried to write a letter. She could think of nothing to say. There was too much to say and nowhere to begin. Abigail desperately needed help but didn't want to impose. Laura might dress in fine gowns and carry herself as a cultured young lady, but she had no money.

None.

Laura would have to ask her husband-to-be, and that probably would not go well. Judging from the man's expression yesterday on the Galveston pier, Laura's intended wasn't inclined to lend money to Laura's friends. Mr. Bailey looked almost as furious as Mr. Walker.

Abigail set her pen aside and crumpled the paper, her third attempt at a letter for Laura. She rose from her chair and returned to pacing the room. Her gown rustled, the sound mocking her every step.

She felt like a fraud in Miss Peabody's dresses. Laura had taken in the bodice on each dress. They fit but they weren't comfortable. Last night, Abigail had ransacked her trunks, looking for her old muslin dresses but to no avail. Finally, after an hour of fruitless searching, she came to the conclusion that Laura had discarded the dresses.

That could be the only explanation.

The notion made sense, considering how Laura had regarded the garments with thinly veiled disgust, muttering that the frocks weren't even good enough to keep as rags. They were worn. Threadbare. Laura was right. The gowns were a poor excuse for a dress. Still, Abigail mourned their loss. The dresses were familiar and comfortable. Not like the costly gowns Miss Peabody had gotten for the trip to Texas.

As the morning wore on, Abigail thought she heard a sound in the baby's room. Had the Walkers left the child behind while they'd gone to breakfast? The idea shocked her. She knew nothing about children, truth be told. She could manage the care of a kitten better than a child, but she knew that a child shouldn't be left unattended. She crept to the nursery to make certain the boy was well.

She didn't find the boy, however. Only a hotel maid.

"Good morning, miss," the girl stammered. "I'm sorry to disturb you. I only wanted to tidy the rooms. I can return later. I thought your family was at breakfast."

Abigail bit her lip. She and the Walkers were hardly a family. It wouldn't do to explain that to the girl, who would likely draw a scandalous conclusion.

"It's no trouble at all," she said, putting on a bit of an act. She waved her hand in what she hoped appeared to be an elegant gesture. "Carry on."

The girl offered a slight curtsey. Abigail turned on her heel and fled the room before she gave herself away. Her stomach clenched. Her throat felt parched and tight. She sipped a cup of lukewarm tea.

"What am I doing?" she muttered. "What on earth am I doing?"

"You're eating breakfast. That's what you're doing."

Abigail cried out in dismay, whirling around to find Eleanor standing in the doorway. "I'm sorry, dear. I didn't mean to startle you."

Eleanor entered the room, followed by a hotel valet pushing a cart. The aroma of bacon, biscuits and eggs wafted through the air. Abigail's stomach rumbled with hunger pangs.

The hotel nursemaid carried the baby into the room. Abigail found she could scarcely tear her eyes from the baby. She moved across the room, hardly aware of her own movements and went to the nursemaid.

The baby looked up at her. His rosebud mouth tilted. A smile curved his lips, revealing toothless gums.

"There's mother," the nursemaid cooed, holding the baby out to her.

Abigail took the baby and felt herself give the boy an answering smile. Justin added an adorable chuckle to his grin. He kicked his legs with a happy little motion. Suddenly Abigail realized the nursemaid thought she was the baby's mother.

"Oh, but I'm not-"

"That's all we'll need," Eleanor said to the girl, dismissing her.

"I'm not the boy's mother," Abigail said.

"No, but you're the first person to coax a smile from the little one."

Eleanor ushered her to a nearby chair, set a bottle in her hand and settled on the chesterfield. She went on about books she'd bought for Abigail to read, and about a Dr. Whitacre who was the boy's doctor.

Abigail only half-listened. Instead, she watched how the child drank his bottle. She studied the way his little fingers curled into a fist. And she noted how his brows knit when the bottle was done.

"Look at you," Eleanor murmured, her eyes misting. "You're the girl we've all prayed for."

Even if Abigail could have summoned an objection, she would have remained silent. Last night, she'd given the boy a bottle but hadn't seen his expression since it was dark. Today was different. She'd watched him and seen his little gestures and expressions. Any argument she'd formed fell away. She couldn't imagine a hired girl caring for this small boy. That wouldn't do, she resolved. That wouldn't do at all.

# Chapter Fourteen

**Caleb**

Wakening in his bed at home in the predawn darkness, Caleb tried to clear his mind.

Something was different.

Something was vastly different.

His thoughts spun as he tried to fathom what on earth could be the matter. His first concern was the baby. Justin was fine. The house was quiet.

At times when he and his men took cattle vast distances on a drive, he'd awaken in the night, lying in his bedroll, unsure where he was. That wasn't the case now. While his men were on a cattle drive, taking a herd to General Fitzhugh's camp, Caleb stayed back.

His mind drifted back to Justin and slowly it dawned on him. Abigail slept in the room beside the baby's, and while that was far, far different from the usual, there was something else he couldn't readily put his finger on.

He rose, said his morning prayers. He washed and donned work clothes and boots in preparation for the day's work. After being gone for several days, there would be plenty to do. What he should have been doing was making a mental list of chores.

Instead, he mulled over the different feel to the morning.

Walking quietly along the length of the hallway, he took his usual time and care to avoid the floorboards that squeaked or creaked. He moved slowly, carrying his boots, picking his way in stockinged feet, making every attempt to be as quiet as possible.

No need to waken the baby. Not this early in the morning.

When he inadvertently took a wrong step and drew a complaint from the floorboards, he grimaced. The noise of the floorboards always sounded five times louder in the quiet of nighttime. He waited. Listening. When the baby didn't make a peep, he continued with more care.

When he reached the top of the stairs, it dawned on him. The reason he felt so different this morning was on account of sleeping the whole night through. He hadn't woken to the plaintive cry of a child in the wee hours of the morning. A wave of dismay washed over him. With a worried glance, he fixed his gaze on the hallway leading to the baby's nursery.

A strong urge came over him. He wanted to hurry to the baby's room and listen as he always did. He yearned to hear the child's soft breathing. And yet, he couldn't exactly prowl down the same hallway where Abigail slept. How would that look to the young lady if she were to emerge from her room and find him standing in the hallway?

He answered his own question. It wouldn't look good. At all.

With a soft grumble of dismay, he assured himself that the child was fine. Of course, he was. Aunt Eleanor was here, sleeping in her room in the same hallway as Abigail and Justin. If there had been a problem of any kind, she would have awoken and alerted him.

Downstairs, he helped himself to a cup of coffee the cook had already brewed and left the house with a sigh of relief.

The business of running a ranch appealed to him, now more than ever. The work was simple. Straightforward. Nothing like the goings-on that transpired in his home.

He spent the morning with his men, culling yearlings from the herd. Under usual circumstances, he'd forgo lunch and spend the day in the pasture. With Abigail in the house, he found it difficult to keep his thoughts from her and Justin. He told himself it was the boy that concerned him the most. Having a young woman in his home was a simple necessity.

The fact that she was lovely didn't factor into his thinking. Her smile and laughter meant nothing, he assured himself. He swore he didn't notice her fragrance very often either.

Returning to the house, he heard her voice on the back porch. He hitched his horse to the post in the front and circled to the gardens. He found Abigail and Eleanor chatting. To his surprise, the baby lay in a cradle in a sunny spot on the porch. Despite the women's conversation, he dozed peacefully.

He swept his hat from his head and greeted the women with a polite nod. "Shouldn't the boy be upstairs, where it's quiet?"

Abigail walked the length of the porch, holding a large volume. "I was just telling your aunt that some children get their days and nights mixed up. It says so in the book she bought for me. 'Dr. Owen's Complete Book of Childcare'."

Eleanor sat on the porch swing, looking smug. "Abigail, the clever girl, has already read half the book."

Abigail flushed with pleasure, seemingly pleased with Eleanor's praise. He allowed himself a lingering gaze at her shy smile. She had a light spray of freckles adorning her milky skin. When she blushed, they grew less distinct, but reappeared as the emotion faded. One by one, like stars in the dusk sky, they returned.

He shook his head, wondering what on earth was wrong with his mind. He'd never given a moment's thought to evening stars, or a woman's freckles. Eleanor regarded him with a widening smile as if she enjoyed his distress immensely.

"Days and nights confused?"

"Abigail's quite clever," Eleanor said.

"So you said." He turned his hat over in his hands, frowning at his aunt.

"We'll have to think of some way to keep her on," Eleanor said. "We'll never find another girl who is so…"

Her words drifted off.

"Clever?" he offered.

He could see her sharp reply forming in her mind. She'd like to fuss at him and tell him not to sass his elders, but likely didn't want to grouse about that topic. Instead, she kept a smile on her lips and maintained a steady gaze square upon him.

"I meant to say that we'd never find another girl who would stay up half the night to read about childcare." Eleanor sniffed. "I happen to approve of that sort of pluck and determination."

"I'm not so sure about pluck and determination," Abigail offered. "I couldn't sleep."

"Don't argue, young lady," Eleanor snapped and then added a few words to soften her reply. "I know a girl of character when I meet her. And character is every bit as important as family and name."

Eleanor's conciliatory words missed their mark. Abigail looked downcast for an instant before replying. "I don't have family or a name that would count for much."

"Exactly," Eleanor said. "You have character, however. And that means a great deal to me."

Abigail blushed and ran her fingers along the fabric of her dress. The boy stirred in his cradle. Without an instant's hesitation, Abigail hurried to the child. Eleanor gave him a pointed look. "She'll have a name soon enough, won't she, Caleb?"

He shook his head and left the women on the porch. Eleanor seemed to think she could issue a proclamation and her wishes would be carried out. He wasn't even sure Abigail wanted to be in Texas, much less caring for a stranger's child. She seemed agreeable now, but how long would that last?

Later in the afternoon, a buggy arrived from Sweet Willow. The buggy belonged to Dr. Whitacre. Eleanor insisted on the doctor visiting every week to offer his assurance that the baby was healthy. She fretted that his constant fussing and crying meant that the boy suffered from some mysterious malady. Deep down, Caleb had the same worries.

Caleb worked in the corral, training a gelding to accept the saddle and bridle. He usually left the task of working with young horses to his men, but he wanted to remain close to the house in case Abigail or Eleanor needed him. It was Abigail's first few days at the ranch, after all.

He stood by the horse, petting its neck as he watched the doctor get out of his buggy and greet the women. One of Caleb's men took the horses to tend to them while the doctor chatted with Eleanor and Abigail.

The doctor, an elderly man with a voice like a bellow, made a fuss over Abigail. Caleb could hear him all the way over in the corral.

"Why, aren't you a pretty little thing."

Caleb tightened his hands around the bridle reins. That Dr. Whitacre was as charming as the day was long. He wasn't untoward, of course. Far from it. Still, it didn't sit well with Caleb that the man was making a fuss over Abigail because when Doc Whitacre got back to town, he'd tell everyone he saw that there was a new girl at the Walker Ranch, and a pretty one at that.

The last thing Caleb wanted was for the men in Sweet Willow to get ideas about Abigail.

Eleanor laughed and patted the doctor on the shoulder. This only fueled Caleb's aggravation. Sometimes he thought Eleanor had a tender spot in her heart for the old doctor. Maybe that's why she insisted he come out to the ranch every week. Maybe it had nothing to do with Justin.

And maybe that was a good thing, the other part of his mind reasoned. If that was the reason the man came each week, it would lend credence to the notion that the baby was perfectly healthy. Caleb considered that idea for a moment and found comfort thinking that the boy didn't suffer from any ailment whatsoever.

It made sense. The boy just needed a tender touch, a mother's care. His heart lurched once more as he realized that Justin had hardly made a peep since Abigail had arrived. Everything seemed different. Everything. He'd been aware of that stark reality from the moment he'd woken that morning.

# Chapter Fifteen

**Abigail**

Abigail held her breath while the doctor examined the child. He listened to the baby's heart and lungs, lifted him in the air a time or two like a little sack of potatoes, pronounced the baby healthy as a horse and gave him back to Abigail.

Abigail had his bottle ready and set about feeding the baby. Although she had only just begun to care for Justin, she found it natural and comforting to hold him in her arms. Why that was, she couldn't say. She'd spent her childhood in an orphanage, but she was the youngest among the children right up until she went to live in the Peabody home. She had no experience with babies. None.

Still, she enjoyed the way the baby molded himself to her shoulder. The way he sank against her brought a smile to her face. She probably looked like a half-witted fool, sitting on the porch swing, rocking a sleeping baby with a smile playing on her lips.

Fortunately, Eleanor didn't notice, or if she did, she said nothing. She was more concerned about chatting with Dr. Whitacre. The two of them seemed like dear friends.

As the afternoon wore on, it became clear that the doctor would stay for an early dinner before returning to Sweet Willow. Eleanor instructed the kitchen staff to set an extra place.

"Would you be a dear, Abigail? Go and fetch Caleb for dinner. I'm sure he'll want to join us for dinner even though it's a tad early."

The baby had awoken and rested comfortably in her arms. Abigail eased the baby out of her embrace and set him in his cradle. He blinked and knit his brow in what struck her as something of an unhappy expression. He didn't want to be set down. He wanted to be held. Abigail stifled a small laugh. Even his little frown delighted her. Everything about the boy gladdened her heart.

"Don't worry, dear," Eleanor said. "I'll be certain to watch over your charge. I'm sure you'll find Caleb in the barn."

Abigail crossed the barnyard and pushed the barn door open. The barn was quiet. She didn't want to simply shout his name. That wouldn't do. She wasn't certain how things were done here on the ranch, but her sense of decorum suggested she find him rather than shout. She still wasn't entirely comfortable calling him by his given name.

She went inside and looked around. Three of the stalls held yearlings. Another one had an older-looking horse. She searched the barn but didn't find Caleb. Just as she was about to leave, a movement caught her attention. It was a cat prowling the length of the barn. Forgetting her task, she tiptoed behind the cat, wondering if perhaps it had a litter of kittens.

The tabby ignored her and stalked after something. The cat didn't have kittens. Perhaps it chased a mouse. His tail twitched as he stared into a shadowed corner. Abigail crept closer, peering into the darkened spot wondering what the cat pursued. The animal gathered its feet under him and pounced. A yowl followed. Then a scuffle. Suddenly a rat dashed from the shadows with the cat in hot pursuit.

Without thinking, Abigail lunged to the side. She found herself clinging to a ladder. The cat raced under her. She scrambled up the ladder with a cry of distress. When she reached the top, she flung herself off the ladder and from the safety of the hayloft, peered down.

Her breathing came fast. A small murmur of distress fell from her lips. Rats. Dear heavens. And to think she'd considered remaining in Texas. Not anymore! She'd take the first ship back to Boston, or anywhere else.

The barn grew quiet. The cat must have left. With luck, the rat had as well. But what if it hadn't? Her heart thundered against her ribs. Her throat, dry as sand, tightened. She tried to swallow the lump of fear to no avail.

"Hello?" she called out, no longer concerned with decorum.

Silence.

She cleared her throat. *"Hello..."*

Another cat strolled into the barn. This one, a pretty calico, looked up at her with vague interest. Abigail left her spot at the top of the ladder and paced the length of the hayloft. The floorboards creaked beneath her boots. At the far end, she spied a small window held shut with a bolt. After some considerable effort, she wrenched it open. Below lay an empty corral.

"Mr. Walker," she called, her voice trembling.

Of course, no one replied. There was no one around. She was alone. Utterly alone. Well, aside from the calico downstairs and possibly a rat. Heavens, what if the rat had friends and extended family?

She returned to the ladder and looked down to find that the cat had indeed remained in the barn. Thank goodness. Not that the cat offered any help. The animal lazed near the bottom of the ladder and took a bath.

"A bath sounds very nice." Abigail sighed. "If I escape this loft, I'll get to enjoy a bath too."

The cat finished its bath and yawned.

Abigail could imagine Eleanor and Dr. Whitacre talking in earnest and forgetting everything in their midst as the sun set. She hoped they would at least remember to take the baby inside. The sun sank to the west. The evening air held a chill. Beams of sunlight shone through the barn slats. They lengthened, dimmed and faded as afternoon gave way to dusk.

"I'm not supposed to be here," Abigail informed the cat. "Oh, I know what you're thinking. I'm not supposed to be in the hayloft. That's quite obvious, I'm sure. What I mean is I'm not supposed to be *here*. As in here on the Walker Ranch, in Texas. I'm here because I was simply trying to do my duty and my mistress felt no compunction in letting me do her dirty work."

The cat flicked its tail.

"Shocking, isn't it? I'm certain she sent me to Texas to explain to your master that she'd had a change of heart. I suppose that was easier than sending a letter. And do you know why it was easier than sending a letter?"

The cat lay still, not even offering a tail twitch.

"Oh, I'll tell you why. It was easier to send me than to send a letter, because she'd used my words for her letters all along. That's why."

The cat rolled onto her back and pawed the air.

"Yes," Abigail replied. "Shocking, yet true."

She lowered to rest on her haunches, not a very ladylike posture but she no longer concerned herself with feminine airs. All she wanted to do was to believe that Eleanor would come look for her. Soon.

Well, that wasn't entirely true. She wanted Eleanor to make certain Justin was safe and sound and *then* come look for her. Eleanor wouldn't have a moment's hesitation when it came to taking on rodents. No, the rats would likely run from her if they knew what was good for them.

Abigail, despite feeling sorry for herself, smiled to imagine Eleanor Walker in this situation. Eleanor would never have clambered up a ladder in fright. Abigail couldn't picture Eleanor being afraid of anything. Wandering back to the window, she stuck her head out and tried to glimpse the house. It was no use, however. The best she could do was see a corner of the porch.

Hopefully, Eleanor would notice her missing and come looking for her. Perhaps she'd send someone. A rustling from above drew a sharp gasp of dismay from Abigail. A dove flew across the span of the barn and alighted on a massive beam. The bird cooed, ruffled her feathers and peered down at Abigail as if resenting the intrusion.

Abigail let out a trembling sigh. Thank goodness it was only a bird and nothing worse. She studied the loft, noting the heaps of hay and tidy, swept passages that lay between the piles. It looked like someone had been up here recently. She glanced up at the bird once more. The creature ignored her now and strutted along the length of the beam and then back again.

The absurdity of her situation struck her once more. Her thoughts flew to Caleb Walker. He regarded her with suspicion. Clearly. He likely imagined that she'd conspired to come to Texas and take Miss Peabody's place. How could she make him believe that her coming here had never been part of her plan?

The unbearable truth was that she'd been hoodwinked at best. At worst, Miss Peabody had betrayed her. Even now, the notion was almost too shocking to believe. And yet, here she was, in Texas, trapped in a hayloft in what appeared to be a rat-infested barn. She let out a small, self-pitying sigh.

Returning to the ladder, she peered down to find the cat still there.

"Sweet kitty," Abigail said softly, rubbing her arms against the evening chill. "Rats don't know how to climb ladders, do they?"

# Chapter Sixteen

**Caleb**

Trying to keep busy, and out of the house, Caleb occupied himself with small chores around the farmyard. With his men gone, some working in the far pastures, some on the Army cattle drive, he enjoyed the solitude. The only problem with the quiet was the way his thoughts wandered.

Usually, in idle moments, he mulled over the child. Worries plagued him about the little boy. Could he manage the boy's upbringing? That was the big question that hung over his head.

Ever since he'd seen her struggling to save the small girl, flailing in the water of Galveston Harbor, his mind whirred with other ideas, thoughts that had nothing to do with the boy in his care. Had that just been a few days ago? Hard to believe.

He grumbled under his breath as he hammered a loose board in the corral. Women had a way of upsetting plans. Getting a mail-ordered bride was supposed to be a help. He'd reread the letters last night, this time imagining the woman who had dictated them. At nineteen, Abigail was scarcely more than a girl. How could he entrust the care of his nephew to a girl who knew so little of children?

Striking the nail with more force than he intended, he hit the head at a wrong angle. In the failing light, he could see clearly that he'd bent the nail. He shook his head. Muttering about his own incompetence, he pried the nail free.

A stray nail was a danger to horses. One of the reasons he liked doing his own repairs. If one of his men let a nail fall to the ground, it could lame a horse, maybe permanently.

With grim determination, he set about driving the last nail into the board. He found comfort in his work and relief thinking about the task at hand. Anything was better than stewing about his bride dilemma. He could just imagine the people of Sweet Willow, chuckling at his expense.

The worst would be Seth Bailey. The man had been there in Galveston. His bride had arrived on the same ship as Abigail's. She'd been the one whose girl had plunged into the water. Caleb wondered how things fared at the Bailey Ranch. Seth was probably enjoying a romantic evening with his new bride while Caleb was out trying to hammer a simple nail into a plank of wood.

The hammer glanced off the head of the nail with a clang. Gritting his teeth, Caleb tapped it upright and drove it in the rest of the way. He rubbed the back of his neck and straightened.

An evening breeze washed over him. It carried the sounds of a woman's voice. He growled. Even in the peace and quiet of dusk, his imaginings ventured to the girl. He trudged to the toolshed to return his hammer and box of nails.

A flutter of white caught his eye. It came from the barn on the other side of the yard. One of his men had left the window to the hayloft open. Well, wasn't that dandy? If they'd had any rain, it would have ruined a fair bit of his hay. If he were to question his men, they'd all deny any wrongdoing. Of course, they would. It was lucky he'd ventured to this side of the yard. If not, the window might have remained open for days.

Another movement stopped him in his tracks. A person appeared in the window. Not any person, but Abigail. Slowly, he lifted his hand, removed his hat and stared in disbelief.

There was something powerfully wrong with his mind. He was hearing things. Seeing things. Maybe he'd have a word with Doc Whitacre. Privately of course. No need stirring up trouble with Aunt Eleanor.

"Mr. Walker, I'm terribly sorry to trouble you."

Caleb blinked. The apparition had most definitely spoken. Which was good, he supposed. He wasn't suffering from delusions. The girl was indeed speaking to him from the hayloft window. The notion came as an immense relief. On the other hand, he could not fathom what the girl was doing in his hayloft.

"Mr. Walker, are you well?"

"Not really," he muttered.

She pursed her lips. He wasn't entirely sure if she'd heard him or not. From the slightly indignant look, he assumed she had.

Lifting her chin, she went on in a prim tone. "Mr. Walker, I'm in need of some assistance."

She'd addressed him by his given name several times since arriving. Now she spoke to him formally. She looked somewhat disheveled. Her hair, normally swept back in a sensible knot, hung askew. Several tendrils had fallen free and framed her lovely face in a way he decided made her even prettier.

"How can I help you, Miss Abigail?"

If she had gone back to calling him Mr. Walker, it seemed only right he should call her Miss Abigail.

"I find myself in a bit of a predicament."

Something about her prim tone amused him. "Yes, ma'am, I'd have to agree."

He hoped he didn't sound too amused. His lips wanted to curve into a smile. A chuckle threatened to erupt from deep in his belly. He might not be the most sensitive man in Sweet Willow, but he was certain now was not the time to laugh at Abigail.

Schooling his features into a no-nonsense expression, he waited for her to go on. This was the first time he'd had her to himself, and while he didn't approve of her wandering around the hayloft, he was in no hurry to end the exchange.

"You see, Aunt Eleanor sent me."

His lips twitched at her mention of Eleanor and her use of the word "aunt". Like Abigail was part of the family. A warmth filled his chest. "I see."

He didn't see anything at all, but it seemed the thing to say. Abigail gave a trembling laugh and brushed her hair from her eyes. "Aunt Eleanor sent me to look for you, Mr. Walker."

Of course, she did. He refrained from saying a word. Aunt Eleanor, the schemer, was pushing him and Abigail together. A few short weeks ago, that would have been unfathomable, but his aunt had changed her mind. The discovery of the sleeping draught in the baby's room had changed everything.

"Why did she send you?" he asked.

"It's time for supper. Or it was time for dinner the better part of an hour ago. Hopefully, they saved us a little something."

She laughed softly, amused at her own joke.

"Hopefully," he replied.

"We should probably go to the house. Before anyone starts worrying."

"Sounds fine. I'll need to close that window."

She nodded. "Would you like me to try?"

"No, ma'am. It's heavy. I'll be right up."

Without waiting for a reply, he strode into the barn, went to the ladder and climbed to the loft. When he got to the top of the ladder, he found her struggling to shut the window.

"Let me do that," he chided. "It's too heavy for you."

He wanted to add that she shouldn't be in the hayloft in the first place but decided against stating the obvious. She stepped away. He pulled the window shut and shoved the wooden bolt in place. Without the light from the window, the hayloft fell into shadows.

"I'm sorry for the trouble." Abigail retreated a step, clasping her hands.

"It's all right." He gestured, spreading his hands wide. "This is the hayloft."

"I assumed so. Judging from all the hay, it was clear that this is indeed the hayloft."

They faced each other, neither moving. Silence filled the loft until the soft coo of a dove wafted through the stillness. Caleb glanced at the main beam and spied a small gap near the roofline. Situated under the roof, it didn't allow rain to fall into the loft, but it did offer enough room for the mourning doves to come in at night to roost.

"If you'd like to see the ranch, I'd be happy to show you around," Caleb said.

"I didn't come up here to sight-see. I came up here to get away from the rats."

Caleb narrowed his eyes. "Rats, you say?"

She nodded. "The cat stalked a rat. Enormous. B-big as my arm."

He growled under his breath. He prided himself on the upkeep of his ranch. How had he ended up with rats?

He gestured to the ladder. "Darn cats aren't earning their keep."

They went to the ladder and paused at the top. He wasn't sure about the etiquette of descending a ladder with a lady. Should he let her go first, or should he go ahead to help her down when she reached the bottom?

"Would you like me to go first, Miss Abigail?"

"Thank you, Mr. Walker. That would be very kind."

He went down and waited a respectful distance from the bottom. He averted his gaze to allow her a private moment as she descended. It couldn't be easy in a dress.

Halfway down, she paused. "Are you sure the rats are gone?"

Seeing her perched on the ladder brought a powerful wave of protectiveness over him. He wanted to wrap his arms around her. A fall from that height might not hurt her, but then again, it might. He moved closer just in case she took a misstep.

"I suppose they might be gone." He didn't really know but it seemed like that might be the thing to say. "I'm not entirely sure there are rats here."

"Mr. Walker, I can assure you I saw a rat."

Her indignant tone made his lips tug into a smile he could no longer resist. From the distance of an arm's length, he caught a hint of her feminine scent. Something floral and delicate that made him want to protect her even more. She was afraid. He could help.

"Miss Abigail, I cannot say for certain if the rats are gone, but if you'd like, I could carry you out of the barn."

Her lips parted. She drew a sharp breath of surprise and regarded him with a fastidious expression. She seemed too surprised to reply.

Were there rats in the barn? He hoped not. On the other hand, it suited his purposes if she thought the barn teemed with dangerous and unpleasant creatures. He'd relish the chance to hold her in his arms even if it meant engaging in a little hint of deception. What was the saying?

All's fair in love and war...

He tried his best to sound indifferent and sensible. "I already carried you out of the Bay of Galveston. I promise to carry you safely away from the threat of rats or any other menace that might be lurking in this barn."

"What will your aunt think if she sees you carrying me out of the barn?"

He shrugged. "She'll simply congratulate herself for raising me to be a gentleman."

Eh. Probably not. Not if she knew he had a few schemes of his own. Eleanor wanted him to court Abigail, of that he was sure, however, she might not approve of his methods. She certainly wouldn't endorse frightening the girl.

"All right," Abigail said quietly.

He set his hat on his head, drew closer, reaching for her with a gentle murmur, meant to ease her dismay. She flinched but allowed him to take her in his arms. When he'd held her soft form the first time, she'd been soaking wet and terrified. Not only that, but he'd had to hold both Abigail and the small girl. The two females were slight but had flailed with confusion and terror.

This time there was no confusion. No terror. Probably no terror. There was definitely alarm, though. He felt the tension in her body as she tried to keep a respectful distance between them. Instead of leaning into his embrace, she looked stiffly away from him, keeping her gaze fixed on some point ahead of them.

When they reached the doorway, he pulled it open with his boot. To his surprise, both Aunt Eleanor and Dr. Whitacre stood on the other side. Eleanor's jaw dropped. Whitacre's brows lifted. It was as if a jolt flowed down Abigail's body as she tried her best to scramble out of Caleb's arms.

"Whoa, there, Miss Abigail," he drawled. "I'll set you down just as soon as you stop struggling."

She went still. The only sound coming from her was an indistinct whimper.

He put her down and brushed off his hands. For a long moment, no one spoke. With eyes as big as plums, Eleanor lifted her hand to Abigail's face. She grasped a stalk of hay that clung to Abigail's disheveled hair. Gently and with slow deliberation, she pulled the hay free and let it fall to the ground.

# Chapter Seventeen

**Abigail**

After returning to the house, Abigail tried to excuse herself from the group. Her cheeks burned with mortification. How must it appear to Eleanor and Dr. Whitacre, indeed the entire household? She'd been gone for over an hour and then was discovered in Mr. Walker's arms. Even worse, it must have looked like she'd been *in* the hay.

She might be a demure and innocent young woman, but she understood full well that both Eleanor and Dr. Whitacre guessed she and Caleb had engaged in something quite untoward. Caleb, she was sure, had found the entire thing amusing.

"I should tend to the baby," she said to Eleanor, scarcely able to meet her eye.

Eleanor held the boy. "Nonsense. Go fix your hair, dear, and make yourself ready for dinner. We'll eat together. All of us. And then you can tell us about your adventure in the hayloft."

Dr. Whitacre's laughter boomed, filling the parlor with deep, mirthful reverberations.

Abigail offered a trembling smile. She fled, rushing upstairs, almost bumping into Caleb Walker on the landing. He returned from his rooms, his face freshly washed, his hair combed neatly.

"You coming back?" he asked as he continued downstairs.

"Yes," she replied.

He glanced over his shoulder, pausing, his expression curious.

"Everything okay, Miss Abigail?"

*Just fine!* She wanted to shout. Absolutely *dandy* – using one of his expressions. *I've been forced to come to Texas, abandoned by my employer, and made to live on a ranch with a group of rough cowboys. Not to mention massive rodents. Couldn't be dandier!*

"I just need to make myself presentable," she said with as much dignity as she could muster.

His lips curved into a smile and he nodded before continuing downstairs.

After she arranged her hair and dress into some semblance of decorum, she hurried back down. Wordlessly, she slipped into her chair across from Eleanor. The baby lay in his bassinet in the corner of the room, gurgling and cooing happily.

The first course had been served, a light vegetable soup. Caleb gave thanks. They began to eat. Dr. Whitacre took a roll from the breadbasket, yelping when the hot bread burned his fingertips. The roll tumbled to the floor.

He pushed his chair back and went under the table to retrieve the roll. Eleanor continued eating, and politely ignored the doctor. Abigail stole a glance at Caleb. He winked at her, setting her cheeks ablaze once more.

The doctor returned to his seat. He grumbled as he tugged his jacket down. "Ah, rats."

Dr. Whitacre gave Abigail a look of feigned innocence. "Sorry about that, little lady." He leaned forward and continued in a conspiratorial whisper. "Didn't mean to mention the word *rats*."

Eleanor chuckled. "Gavin, you're terrible."

Abigail gave Caleb an accusing glare, but he didn't meet her eye. He didn't smile or chuckle at the doctor's antics.

As dinner progressed, Abigail sensed that the doctor's teasing troubled Caleb. She wasn't sure why that was, but there was no doubt Caleb was displeased. Later, as she took Justin upstairs, she heard Caleb ask the doctor to keep the story of Abigail's misadventure to himself.

"I don't need the good people of Sweet Willow to gossip about Abigail."

The doctor assured Caleb he wouldn't discuss the matter. "It wouldn't do for anyone to call the girl's virtue into question."

Eleanor had quite a bit to say to that, but Abigail couldn't hear much more of the discussion.

Abigail didn't know a single soul in Sweet Willow. Not really, not aside from Laura and Francine and the members of the Walker household. She couldn't imagine being the topic of conversation among perfect strangers. Still, the notion made her feel embarrassed all over again.

She tried to push the thoughts away. Instead of thinking about her own troubles, she prepared the baby's bath. Last night, Eleanor had helped her. This evening, she intended to manage on her own. The upstairs maid filled the small tub with warm water and when she left, Abigail undressed the boy.

Justin's mouth tugged into a smile as he gazed at her. She stopped and stared in amazement.

"You have dimples, young man," she murmured, offering a smile in return.

He kicked his legs, pumped his arms and widened his smile.

A sound came from behind her.

"Eleanor," she said, without taking her eyes from the baby. "Our little fellow is smiling again."

The footsteps drew closer and the heavy footfall told her it was Caleb who had come.

He moved to her side. "Why, look at that. He's quite the little charmer, isn't he? Usually, he's hollering loud enough to wake the dead."

"Look at his dimples." She glanced up at Caleb. A few moments ago, she'd been too mortified for words. Now in the quiet of the bathroom, with Justin giving them smiles, her discomfort faded. Unable to resist teasing Caleb, she asked, "Are those a Walker trait?"

He shook his head. "Not this Walker. His dimples must come from his mama's side of the family. Maybe he'll get lucky and get her good looks too."

Abigail flushed as much at his tone as his words. He spoke softly, gently. The awkwardness of their mishap in the barn drifted further from her mind. Caleb might be seeking a compliment or two but at least he wasn't teasing her. Not like Dr. Whitacre.

If she'd been a tad braver, she might have confessed that she thought Caleb was handsome from the moment she first saw him, or almost from the start. Her first meeting with the man had been in the frigid waters of the bay. She'd hardly had the opportunity to admire his looks. After she was safe and sound, not to mention dry, she'd thought he was fine-looking indeed. Not at all the elderly, portly man she'd pictured on her way to Texas.

He held her gaze. She turned away to avoid looking into his eyes. Instead, she finished undressing the baby.

"Would you like to set him in his bath?" she asked.

"Me?"

"Yes. You."

"He's so small." Caleb held up his hands. "I'm always afraid I'll hurt him."

"You're strong. But your touch is gentle."

This time it was his turn to get embarrassed. His cheeks pinked. He gave her a look that bordered on stern. "We best not mention that to anyone. I don't want anyone to suggest anything untoward."

"Nor do I." She replied hastily, regretting her attempt to make light of what had happened. "Why don't you put him in the tub?"

Caleb lifted the boy and lowered him into the water. Justin chortled. His face lit with happiness.

"I think the child likes a bath," she suggested, rubbing the soap on a cloth.

"Maybe he gets that from me."

Abigail bit her lip, stealing a quick glance at his expression. His cheeks were still tinged with pink. He looked sheepish. "It's true. The guest bathroom has a fine bathtub, one the first owners imported from England. I like to take a soak in there. One day when he's grown a little, Justin might like to do the same."

"The tub by my room?"

"That's the one."

The tub he referred to sat in a large bathroom next to her room. The bathroom was immense, bigger than her bedroom in the Peabody home. The tub dominated the room, taking up most of the wall under a large window. She could well imagine the tub might accommodate his tall, muscular frame. A thread of warmth moved across her skin. It wasn't decent to imagine a man soaking in a tub but nothing about their living arrangements was proper.

"I'm sorry I took your tub from you, Mr. Walker," she said, a smile edging her words.

"Don't give it a thought, Miss Abigail. Anyway, the tub was brought to Texas for the lady of the house."

"The lady of the house? I'd always imagined this home belonged to a bachelor."

The moment the words left her lips, she realized how absurd they must sound. The truth, she realized, was that she hadn't wanted to think of the house in any other way. One day, Caleb would take a wife, a woman who would care for Justin. The baby's smiles, as well as Caleb's smiles, would be for a stranger, not her.

Caleb folded his arms. "This house was built for a woman."

"You don't say." She scrubbed the baby's tummy a little more firmly than she intended. He squirmed and chuckled, an adorable sound that chased her sad thoughts away.

Caleb laughed too. "Why, you made the little fellow give a belly laugh. I've never heard him make that sound."

"He's ticklish."

"As I was saying, the house was built for a woman."

"And that's the reason for the enormous tub. She must have been fond of her bath."

"No one knows."

Abigail drew a startled breath. "What happened? She died a tragic death?"

"No, ma'am. Her husband, a wealthy shipping merchant, built the house in the 1840s. He intended to come to Texas to raise a family from up north somewhere. The day his wife arrived along with six stagecoaches, she had a terrible fright. She saw some kind of critter she'd never seen before, turned right around and got back on the stagecoach."

"My word," Abigail exclaimed. "What sort of animal did she encounter?"

When he didn't reply, she looked up from her task. He blinked, pressed his lips into a thin line but didn't reply. His gaze shifted. He cleared his throat.

"Mr. Walker?"

"Miss Abigail?"

She returned her attention to the baby, rinsing the suds from his shoulders and arms. He wriggled. The water pleased him very much, not like some of the babies in the book Eleanor had assigned her. So many of the instructions pertained to children who didn't care for bath time. Clearly, Justin would not be fussy in that regard.

She continued washing the child until she'd assured herself that she'd rinsed every bit of soap from his soft skin. The baby care book devoted an entire chapter to the care of a baby's delicate skin. The author made the point several times that a child's skin should be kept scrupulously clean but cautioned that soap residue would irritate a baby and cause him to wake at night.

When Caleb didn't reply, and she sensed his growing hesitation, she sighed. "You can tell me. I'm not such a delicate female that I can't know the details."

He coughed and cleared his throat again. "The trouble is, you see, I don't recall what sort of animal she came across. Maybe it was a cat. Probably. Or a kitten. Some folks just don't care for cats, ever noticed? They either like dogs or they like cats, but rarely both. Funny thing how some folks are around... a kitten."

"A kitten?" she remarked skeptically.

"Anyway, we're all mighty glad you're here."

He evaded her question. A kitten? Did he think she'd believe that? The last thing she wanted to do was press him on the matter. What if the mystery animal was even worse than a rat? The indignity of the afternoon was still fresh in her mind. She dropped the topic of the creature that had frightened off the first lady of the house.

Clearly Caleb had no intention of telling her the details. Pushing the thought aside, she assured herself she'd never have any trouble with Texas critters, especially if she stayed clear of the barn.

"If you're done, I can lift him out for you," Caleb offered.

He took the baby from the bath and set him on the table beside the small tub.

"Thank you." She took a towel from a nearby shelf and dried the baby.

Caleb grabbed another towel and draped it across the child's lower body. "Trust me, Miss Abigail, you want to keep him covered. I might not know a lot about babies, but I can tell you from experience, Justin's got perfect aim."

She laughed. Caleb laughed along with her, as did the baby. A soft warmth filled her chest. If only she could hold onto this moment, pack it away deep in her heart and keep it forever.

"I should just ask you to marry me," he said.

His words send a jolt of surprise down her spine. "I can't. I have to return to Boston. I made a promise to Miss Peabody's family."

"What sort of promise?"

"To care for her, to stay with her until she married or…"

"Or what?"

"Or until she went on..." Abigail's words trailed off. She drew a deep breath to continue. "Until she went on to her reward."

Caleb recoiled. "Until she *died*?"

The disbelief in his tone took her aback.

"That's right," she whispered. "I was only fifteen when I made the promise. I felt certain I owed the family a debt. They'd lifted me from poverty and ignorance, fed and clothed me. Gave me a home. How could I say no?"

"They were wrong to ask." Caleb's eyes sparked with a slow burn of anger. "You were just a child."

Abigail felt compelled to defend the Peabody family. Words failed her. A man like Caleb Walker couldn't possibly know what it meant to be so indebted. To have so few opportunities. To feel so beholden.

He went on. His voice a low growl. "Old Whitacre gossips worse than anyone in town." Caleb raked his fingers through his hair. "Before you know it, every young buck in Sweet Willow is going to come courting."

"I can't stay." She lifted her chin. "I made a promise and I intend to keep it."

"Nobody's going to care about a promise you made to a fool-headed woman who not only lied and cheated but also sent you alone to Texas to take the blame."

Abigail held the baby close, tucking him under her chin and fixed her gaze upon Caleb. For a long moment, they regarded each other, both with dismay and ire. The stubborn man wanted to make her change her mind. She could not forget her promise, come what may. She'd have to leave the precious child behind. It was a heart-wrenching truth. She had no choice.

Finally, he turned and left the room. His footfalls echoed in the hallway, fading into the quiet of early evening.

# Chapter Eighteen

**Caleb**

In the past, Caleb had made the trip into Sweet Willow to attend Sunday services with a caregiver to help him with Justin. He refused to leave the child at home. It would have been easier for him, as well as the rest of the congregation, for the baby cried and fussed for almost the entire time.

Abigail had been with them almost two weeks the first time he took his family to Sunday services. They'd missed the first Sunday. The river had flooded making the trip impossible, but the second Sunday offered fine weather. Caleb hitched the buggy, helped Eleanor, Abigail and the baby get situated and they set off.

In Church, Caleb sat beside his aunt but stole glances at Abigail when he could. She sat serenely, a sweet smile playing on her lips as she listened to the pastor's sermon. She wore an elegant navy dress, somber but delicate. He supposed it was something Harriet Peabody had bought for herself. He couldn't help smiling to think that Abigail had taken the dress and made it her own.

Another thing that pleased him immensely was the blessed peace and quiet. Instead of squalling, the boy simply dozed or looked around with interest. In the short time Abigail had cared for Justin, she'd worked nothing short of a miracle. The boy no longer cried plaintively. Now he smiled and even laughed.

The other parishioners smiled with approval. They too were grateful for Justin's new ways. Their eardrums had suffered plenty.

They visited a short while after services. Abigail searched for a sight of Laura, eager to hear how she and Francine fared, but saw no sign of them. She'd been so busy with her own situation that she hadn't sent a note. She promised herself that she'd remedy that soon.

After the crowds began to thin, they boarded the buggy and returned to the ranch. Caleb helped Abigail down, letting his hands linger on her waist as long as he dared. The last thing he wanted was to give the girl any cause for alarm. Eleanor handed the baby down to him and he passed the boy to Abigail right away.

"Are you afraid to hold your own nephew?" she asked, a teasing smile on her lips.

"Maybe a little. I don't do as well as you do. I don't have your tender touch. You're the only one who can calm him."

*Which is why you must forget your promise to Harriet Peabody.*

"I could sit with you this afternoon and show you how to soothe him when he frets."

"Don't agree to her plan," Eleanor said. "I won't allow Abigail to leave."

Caleb turned to find that his aunt was in earnest. She looked put upon. Vexed even. He held out his hand to help her down from the buggy. She waved it away.

"I think I'm in trouble," Caleb said under his breath.

"I thought it was me," Abigail replied.

He drove the buggy to the barn and unhitched the team. Eleanor waited until he'd tended to the horses before speaking her mind.

"How long are you going to wait before you offer for the girl?" she demanded.

"I've asked her," Caleb replied with irritation. "She seems to think she owes Harriet Peabody more years of service."

Eleanor wrinkled her nose. "Didn't that woman marry the man who'd jilted her?"

He shrugged. "No way of knowing."

"You're joking. Do you mean to say she intends to leave that baby behind to attend to a woman in Boston? And then what? Read to her? Be a lady's *companion*?"

"It's what she's always done."

Eleanor knit her brow. "To be clear, you did propose marriage to Abigail, right?"

"Yes."

His aunt arched a brow.

"Yes, ma'am."

"And when, precisely, did you ask for her hand in holy matrimony?"

Caleb felt his heart give a slight sinking feeling. He knew he needed to proceed carefully, for Eleanor was clearly on a warpath, likely to find fault with whatever answer he gave. She wasn't used to her plans going awry, and she'd made it abundantly clear that she wanted Abigail to stay to marry him. No matter how much his aunt wished for that to happen, he yearned for it a hundred times more. He examined a bridle, rubbing the worn threads.

"I ought to mend that," he muttered.

"You ought to give me an answer, young man," she snapped. "I can't stay on forever, acting as chaperone to you two."

"I asked her several days ago." He crossed his arms. "I asked her the first few days she was here. While she gave Justin a bath."

Eleanor set her hand on her chest, widened her eyes and, to make perfectly clear that his reply had surprised her, she swayed on her feet and gave a small, piteous murmur. She closed her eyes and lifted a trembling hand to her forehead. Muttering, she rubbed her temples. "Where did I go wrong? Military schools. Nannies. Etiquette classes. Debutante balls. Where. Did I go. Wrong?"

"All those things worked for my brother. Not me. I just wanted to raise cattle and spend my day in the fresh air and God's country."

She groaned dramatically. He waited. She drew a deep breath and slowly opened her eyes. "All right. Let's consider how this went. Perhaps your romantic proposal can be salvaged. Did you bend your knee?"

"No."

Her eyes flashed.

"No, ma'am."

"Did you take her hand in yours?"

"No, ma'am."

Her shoulders slumped a notch. "And what sort of ring did you offer?"

He rubbed the palm of his hand across his chin only to discover he'd forgotten to shave that morning. It was a tad surprising Eleanor hadn't raised heck about that oversight. Clearly, she wasn't in top form. He considered pointing that out but thought better of the reckless notion.

"You..." she whispered. "You didn't offer her a ring, did you?"

"No, ma'am," he replied quietly.

A slow smile spread across her lips. She shook her head and got a faraway look in her eyes as if she might begin to cry. Caleb waited. Wondering. He'd never seen this particular expression on her face and couldn't fathom what had brought it on.

She drew close, stopping right before him. With a smile that bordered on delirious, she chuckled and cupped his jaw. He half-wondered if she'd go off on him about his slovenly habits. But no. He was fairly certain her words would head an entirely different direction.

"We've discovered the problem, haven't we, my darling boy?"

It had been a fair number of years since he'd heard that particular endearment. He winced and hoped like heck she would never call him darling boy in front of his men or Abigail.

"I'm not sure what you're getting at, Aunt Eleanor."

She pursed her lips. A sad, almost tragic expression filled her eyes. She tsked. "Isn't it abundantly clear? The problem is you didn't have a *ring*."

He cupped her hands in his and gave them a quick squeeze. Part of him wanted to laugh at her simple explanation, but the subject was too dear to his heart. He couldn't summon much of a smile.

"You think the problem is the lack of a ring?"

She waved her hand dismissively as if he were toying with her. "Of course, that's the problem. It is, however, an excellent problem to have. I happen to have a small selection of rings with me. Nothing terribly fancy, mind you. My best things are in the safe. You know how it goes with help these days. You can't spend your days counting the silver, can you?"

"No, ma'am." He had no idea what she referred to but could guess the correct reply.

"Heavens, what a relief. My word, I thought the girl might actually get back on a ship and sail off. She even went so far as to ask me for a small loan in order to buy a ticket for next month."

Caleb's shoulders tensed. "You didn't give her the money, did you?"

"Of course not." She tucked her arm around his as they walked out of the barn. "I told her I didn't have a penny to spare. I'm certainly not going to lend her money to buy a ticket for passage back to her dreary life. I'm so relieved to have discovered the trouble. To think you proposed without a ring." She shook her head with relieved bemusement.

Caleb wanted to tell her that a girl like Abigail didn't hold out for jewels. Pricey, sparkling baubles wouldn't change the girl's mind. He considered explaining that Abigail was different than so many of the girls Eleanor had tried to push at him.

His attention was drawn to a new situation, however. Standing in front of his home was a man on horseback, a young child on a pony and several dogs that he'd never seen before. The dogs barked when they saw him, but the man ordered them to be quiet.

"Who is that?" his aunt asked.

As they drew closer, the man dismounted and removed his hat.

"It's Noah Bailey," Caleb explained. "My neighbor's brother. I can't imagine what he's doing here."

"Good afternoon." Noah nodded at Caleb and offered Eleanor a polite smile. "Ma'am."

Before Caleb could ask why Noah had come, Abigail emerged from the house. Her arrival pushed Caleb's protectiveness up a notch, especially when Noah turned to face her. The man's expression softened with obvious admiration. Caleb had the urge to give him a rude shove and send him on his way. He wanted to shield Abigail from the man's gaze, or any man's gaze for that matter.

"Hello there, miss," Noah said. "I believe you know my companion."

He pointed to a boy riding a pony. The child nodded in greeting.

Abigail's brow knit. "I do?"

"Yes, ma'am. This here is Frankie."

The child was already clambering down from the saddle.

"Frankie?" Abigail asked. "I don't know a Frankie. And who are you?"

"Pardon my manners. I'm Noah Bailey, Caleb's neighbor."

The child ran up the stairs. Abigail shrieked, grabbed the child and spun him around in a circle. "Francine! Look at you. I thought you were a boy."

"Heavens," Eleanor murmured. "Is that a girl? Wearing trousers?"

The child swept off her hat to reveal two neat braids tied off with bright pink ribbons. She grinned. "I'm Frankie when I'm a cowgirl."

Abigail let out a cry of shock. "And you're a *talking* cowgirl."

"That's right. Laura's made me pants and shirts so I could ride my pony. I haven't barely even worn a dress."

"My goodness." Abigail shook her head with amazement. "Francine has certainly come around."

"Frankie," the girl corrected. "'Cept for Sundays when Uncle Seth says I need to wear a dress to dinner."

Noah scoffed. "The minute we put Francine in a saddle, she started jabbering away. Most times, none of us can hardly get a word in edgewise."

"That's my pony," Francine said. "I ride the pastures with Uncle Seth. And I help Uncle Noah with the dogs. We came on account of the rats. Everyone's talkin' about how scared you were and how you got trapped in the barn. I told everyone how you don't like rats on account of all the rats at the orphanage."

Abigail turned to give Caleb a look that was partway between mortification and accusation.

He shrugged. There was no way of knowing who had gone to town and blathered the details of the rat incident. It might have been Dr. Whitacre despite Caleb's request that he keep the story to himself. For as much as he knew, the news could have come from his aunt. It didn't much matter now that the Bailey bunch knew about Abigail's misadventure. From this point, the story would spread far and wide.

The small girl kept on, unaware of Abigail's distress. She tugged Abigail's hand to lead her down the steps. "These dogs are rat terriers. The big one's Queenie. The dark one's Duchess and the little one is a runt because she was borned the smallest of the pack and so since she's the smallest, Uncle Noah decided it would be a good idea to call her Princess but sometimes I just call her Tiny."

"My word," Eleanor murmured. "She talks a mile a minute. Most impressive. That little girl could work an auction house."

The girl flicked her braids over her shoulders and gave Abigail a knowing expression, one filled with authority and determination. "Me and Uncle Noah rode over here soon as we heard about the rat problems. We're going to clean up all the rats so you won't be scared anymore and then you won't wanna go back to Boston and anyways you don't wanna go back there because... well, you know?"

"Know what?" Abigail asked warily.

"Hoo – you remember what happened?"

Abigail colored. "Remember what?"

"How you were sick the whole first four days, hunched over with your head in a pail, making those turrible sounds, sick to your stomach and how Laura said you'd been so bad off you were prolly throwing up the vittles from next week. Remember?"

Abigail's lips parted and she began to reply but her words trailed off to nothing.

"I don't think you should get back on *The Sparrow*," Francine said. "I think it's a turrible idea. Specially since you won't have Laura or me."

"What a clever child," Eleanor remarked. She turned to Caleb to add, "Sea travel is so uncivilized. I strongly advise all my friends to avoid journeying by ship if it can be avoided."

The girl chattered on. And on.

Noah smirked and shook his head.

The dogs lay down to rest while the girl went on about Laura and Uncle Seth and the animals at the Bailey ranch, naming them one by one. She circled back to Laura's baking and cooking skills, which were no good at all. Finally, after an uninterrupted stream of news, she paused, looking around at the group as if to notice her audience for the first time.

"Hi." She nodded at Caleb and Eleanor.

Caleb smiled at her greeting. He half-expected her to take off again and talk a blue streak, but she seemed to have run out of steam.

Eleanor gave her a smile. "Very pleased to meet you, Frankie."

# Chapter Nineteen

**Abigail**

Abigail sank into the warm water of her tub. Although she bathed every night, she always marveled at the notion. The Walker home had more help than the Peabody home and the girls were always happy to fill the tub for her. Still, it seemed decadent.

Even Miss Peabody only had a hip bath. This tub was three times the size. Abigail could stretch out fully and not touch the other end with her toes.

In Boston, she bathed in a basin. It was deep, but certainly didn't compare to a bathtub. She'd have to stand in water that came halfway to her knee and wash as quickly as possible. There was certainly no lingering like she did in her Texas tub.

The end result was as different as night and day. In Boston, she'd try to finish before her teeth started chattering. In Texas, she soaked until the water began to slowly chill which took considerably more time than her small basin in Boston. By the time she finished, she felt as self-indulgent and spoiled as a wealthy Boston heiress.

The thought had made her smile, but tonight her mind drifted to the notice in the paper she'd discovered in the sitting room. The newspaper featured an advertisement for a ship traveling in two weeks' time back to Boston. It wasn't the ship she'd come to Texas on, but it didn't matter.

She dressed in a gown and robe. The paper lay on her bedside table. With a heavy heart, she studied the details of the voyage. Although she'd discovered the paper the day before yesterday, she hadn't summoned the courage to ask Caleb for a small loan.

Every time she thought she might have the nerve to broach the subject, she'd lose heart. The prospect of leaving filled her with profound melancholy. She resolved to pay Laura a visit. Perhaps she could bring herself to ask her for help buying a ticket.

The floorboards creaked down the hallway. She crept to the door and opened it. Her heart leapt to her throat. A shadowy figure lurked outside the baby's door. Without thinking, she flew from her room and hurried down the hall. The floor creaked and squeaked and protested beneath her bare feet.

As she drew close, she made out the figure of Caleb Walker, his ear pressed to the door of the nursery. He turned with his brow knit in a frown. Coming to an abrupt halt, she realized with dismay that she stood before him in her gown and robe.

"What are you doing, Mr. Walker?" she whispered.

"I'm checking on the boy."

"Don't go in there. He'll waken."

"I know that." Irritation edged his words. "I never go in there. I just listen so I can make sure he's breathing."

To make sure he was breathing? Abigail wasn't sure what to say to that. It hadn't occurred to her to worry about the boy's breathing. She'd have to search the baby book and see if it mentioned any troubles on this topic.

Caleb leaned toward the door to listen. She held her breath and waited for what seemed an interminable length of time. Finally, exasperated, she blurted, "well?"

"Shh. He's fine."

He moved away from the door, took her elbow and led her down the hall.

"You frightened me," she said. "Why are you checking on his breathing?"

"I do that every night."

"Maybe I should check on him. Did Dr. Whitacre recommend that you should make certain the boy is breathing? What would you do if he weren't breathing? Dear heavens, I can't imagine such a thing."

"He didn't recommend anything. He doesn't know I do that. Nobody knows, except now you do."

In the darkened hallway, she couldn't see his face. He was just a large, shadowed form but she could hear the smile in his voice. He sounded a little sheepish, embarrassed at having been found fretting about the boy.

The sight of him at the nursery door had frightened her at first but as she considered the notion, she found it endearing. Caleb was gruff and often overbearing. He oversaw his immense ranching operation with steely determination by day. And at night, he worried about the small boy in his charge.

"Your secret is safe with me," she said softly.

"Good. Thank you."

"On one condition."

"What?"

"I want to know what the wife saw."

"Come again?"

"The woman who had set out to live here when her husband built the house. What did she see from the stagecoach window?"

He chuckled. "Has that been troubling you, Miss Abigail?"

"Of course, it has. I'm not so gullible to believe she saw a kitten."

She waited, not moving from her spot in front of her bedroom door, hoping he'd tell her what was so terrible that a woman would refuse to set foot from the stagecoach. Abigail had made the trip to Texas and knew how arduous the journey was. She couldn't imagine not wanting to leap from the stage at the first chance. The cramped quarters would be even more oppressive than that of a ship.

The quiet stretched between them. In the distance, a ghostly noise threaded the silence. Was her mind playing tricks on her? The sound, a plaintive howl, grew louder.

"Speak of the devil," Caleb muttered.

"What?"

He pushed her bedroom door open and went inside. Too stunned to protest his untoward behavior, she found herself following him into her room. Moonlight filled the room with a soft, silvery light. He moved to the window and opened it.

Something, or someone wailed. The sound grew louder. More cries joined in. Yipping and screeching rent the air.

"The woman saw a coyote, or so the story goes," Caleb explained. "Now that's not so unusual round these parts, but this one strolled around middle of the day. The bad part? He was foaming at the mouth."

"Oh. My." Abigail felt lightheaded.

"You know what that means, right?" Caleb asked. "When an animal's acting funny and foaming at the mouth?"

"I don't know why that might happen," she said weakly. "But please don't tell me."

Another peal of wild shrieks filled the air. The cries seemed to come from a nearby field. Whatever was out there drew near the house. The moonlight lit the pastures with a bright glow. She might well have been able to glimpse the monstrous creatures if she had dared to look for them.

A woman's voice came from behind her. "Enjoying the moonlight?"

Abigail let out a cry of astonishment. She whirled around to find Eleanor standing in the doorway.

"It's lovely, isn't it?" Eleanor drawled, entirely unconcerned about the wicked sounds coming from outside.

She continued. "So romantic. Drat those coyotes. They know just how to ruin a romantic moment."

She moved past Abigail, nudged Caleb out of the way and closed the window. "I despise coyotes. Mangy, filthy creatures that slink around. Have you ever seen one, darling?"

The best Abigail could manage was a trembling murmur.

"I'll take that as a no. I hope you never do. I wanted to mention something."

"Not now, Aunt Eleanor," Caleb said with a sigh.

"Oh, shush. If she's fond of the emeralds, she must take the matching bracelet. Silly me. I neglected to bring the bracelet along, but it would look simply divine on her wrist." Eleanor turned to address her. "Abigail, my dear, if you like, we can even get my jeweler to make a necklace to match."

Abigail sank to the edge of her bed. What could Eleanor mean by talking about emeralds and necklaces and jewelers? More importantly, what on earth had uttered that eerie cry out in the night? A coyote was akin to a fox or wolf as far as she knew, but the sounds coming from the darkness were more like something from a terrible dream. A nightmare. Maybe that was it.

"I must be dreaming," she muttered. With a sigh, she sank back to her pillows and tugged the blankets over her shoulder.

Eleanor came to her bedside and smoothed the blankets around her. "Look, the poor dear. You've worn her out with your talk of coyotes and such, Caleb. I'm a little disappointed, frankly. You could be whispering sweet nothings. Instead, you're giving a veterinary lecture. What am I going to do with you? I'll have to take matters into my own hands. That's what I'll have to do. I've promised to chaperone but now I'm going to be the opposite of a chaperone."

She left the room, grumbling all the way down the hall. Her voice faded. Abigail closed her eyes and pretended to be asleep. The coyotes had moved on, or perhaps finished their bloodcurdling cries.

"Good night, Miss Abigail," Caleb said. "It was lovely chatting with you."

"Good night, Mr. Walker. Chatting with you was certainly not what I expected." She smiled, opened her eyes and stole a quick glance his way. "It never is."

He laughed softly and left the room, shutting the door gently behind him.

# Chapter Twenty

**Caleb**

Caleb returned home after spending the day searching for a bull that had busted through the fence. It seemed he'd been gone for longer than just a day, he realized as the house came into view. He rode up the hill. A pleasant warmth filled his thoughts as he imagined spending the evening with Abigail.

Dr. Whitacre's buggy sat by the barn. Eleanor still insisted the doctor come once a week to examine the baby.

Abigail sat with the baby on a blanket under the oak trees by the house. Caleb left his horse with one of his men and walked to the oak grove. Abigail smiled at him as he approached. Justin lay on his stomach, pushing himself up off the blanket.

"Look at the boy," Caleb marveled. "He's getting stronger every day."

"Dr. Whitacre said to be sure I put him on his tummy. He fussed at first but less so now."

Caleb glimpsed at the baby book she carried everywhere. A newspaper clipping stuck out of the corner, serving as a bookmark. He saw the print, recognized it as an announcement of a ship coming to Galveston.

"The boy's doing well. He hardly cries anymore." Caleb took off his gloves. "Which is why you can't go back to Boston."

Her smile faded. "I have to return."

He shrugged. "I can't keep you from leaving."

"No..." She gave him a wary look. "I should think not."

"And you can't keep me from getting on that ship with you."

The blood drained from her face. His words were rude and lacking in civility. He didn't care to play at acting the gentleman, not when Abigail was considering real plans for leaving.

"What do you owe Harriet Peabody, exactly?"

Abigail picked up the baby and set him on her lap. She trailed her fingers across his hair. Caleb couldn't imagine the baby sitting with anyone else, not with that contented look on his face.

"When I was nine, I went to work in a girls' school, mopping the floors of the dining hall and cleaning the students' dormitories. I also swept the walkways around the school. It was there that I met Miss Peabody. She was crying, sitting by herself by the gardens. She'd go there every day because the other children were unkind."

Caleb nodded, a tacit encouragement for her to go on.

"Miss Peabody was several years older than me, but soon considered me her friend." Abigail winced. "Her only friend. Her parents were devoted to her. She was an only child. They arranged for me to live with them in their home. They took me in, offered me a life I could never have at the orphanage. In return, they only asked that I serve as a faithful companion to Miss Peabody."

"You can't live your life for her."

"She needs me. I owe the Peabody family more than I can every repay."

"We need you. Besides, she might be married to that rascal that jilted her."

"True. But I have to be sure. Mr. Peabody put a large sum of money into an account for me. The funds serve a sort of contract. I can't break a promise."

Caleb growled softly, slapping the gloves against his palm. He could offer to reimburse Harriet Peabody. It didn't matter how much money it was. He'd pay it. Gladly. But he could tell that Abigail wouldn't have any of that.

"Guess we're going to Boston," he grumbled. "Hope we're not both pukin' at the same time."

Abigail's cheeks pinked. The corners of her lips twitched. "Mr. Walker," she chided.

"I'm not kidding around, Miss Abigail." He gave her an answering smile. "My aunt's dearest wish was that I'd serve on a Navy ship. She wanted me to have a military career more than anything. Her father went to Annapolis. She thinks military service is the finest thing any man could do. Shoot, if the Navy accepted women, she'd have joined and probably been an admiral by now."

Abigail laughed.

Justin squirmed in her lap. Caleb held out his hands to take the boy so Abigail could get to her feet. Caleb expected the baby would cry when he held him but to his surprise, the child did nothing of the sort. Abigail gathered the blanket and draped it over her arm. Side by side, they walked back to the house, their shadows stretching out in front of them in the late afternoon sunshine.

"You going to take care of me on that boat, Miss Abigail?"

"I shall do my best, Mr. Walker. What will the other passengers think of an unmarried man and woman traveling together?"

"Once we're at sea, the captain can marry us."

She laughed softly. "Won't that be romantic?"

"Not if we're both sick as dogs."

The sound of arguing greeted their ears as they ascended the steps to the house. Inside, they found Eleanor and Dr. Whitacre engaged in lively debate. The subject revolved around opening letters addressed to others.

"It is against the law to open mail belonging to other people," Dr. Whitacre said, his voice raised.

"Why must you be such a fuddy-duddy, Gavin?"

"Why must you be such a criminally inclined busybody?"

To this, Eleanor responded with a snort. Caleb and Abigail went to the study where they found Eleanor circling the chesterfield. Dr. Whitacre pursued her, red-faced and filled with outrage.

"You see?" he demanded of Caleb. "Your aunt moves quite well without the cane. She only uses it to inspire sympathy."

"Not true," Eleanor exclaimed. "My leg happens to feel fine. Today." She held up an envelope, waving it in the air, smiling at Caleb. "Something came for you, darling. Shall I open it?"

"The edge is already torn," Caleb replied.

Eleanor and Dr. Whitacre paused, both peering at the envelope. Eleanor turned it over in her hand. The doctor craned his neck from his position across the chesterfield.

"Eleanor," Dr. Whitacre chided. "How could you?"

"Me?" she demanded with her voice edged with indignation. "It was torn when it arrived. Don't blame me. I didn't tear the envelope. It must have been the postman. I've always known that the Sweet Willow post office is full of brigands and swindlers." She narrowed her eyes. "This letter is from Harriet Penobscot."

A gasp fell from Abigail's lips. "Penobscot? She's married?"

"Open it," Caleb said. "Read it aloud."

Before he'd finished, Eleanor had the envelope torn the rest of the way. She cleared her throat and began to read in a dramatic tone.

*Dear Mr. Walker,*

*By now you've met and become acquainted with my companion and servant...*

Eleanor pressed her lips together. "Servant?"

She seethed with anger over the words. For a long moment, Caleb wondered if she might refuse to read any more. She drew several deep breaths, her hand upon her heart and after a long moment, she went on.

*I'm sure she informed you of my change in plans. I'm sorry for any inconvenience. In the hopes of making some small amends, I've sent Abigail to explain matters and to help you with chores. Please accept her service as payment for anything I owe you and send her back when her help is no longer needed.*

Eleanor snorted. "Send her back? Never."

*I hope she is able to serve your household with the same devotion she served here or at least adequately. She is in possession of a number of my own personal belongings. As it will be impossible to return them, please garnish her wages and send me funds in the amount of eighty-four dollars and twenty-three cents.*

Eleanor scoffed and tossed the letter aside angrily. "The nerve of the woman. First, she abandons Abigail and then she decides the poor girl should compensate her for her lost belongings."

Caleb stood rooted to the spot, not sure if now was the time to express relief or happiness. Harriet Peabody was now Harriet Penobscot. He was no longer beholden to her in any way. Even better, neither was his sweet Abigail.

Abigail moved to a nearby chair and slowly sat on the edge. She stared at a vague spot on the floor. After a moment of dazed silence, she rubbed her forehead as if trying to calm the turmoil in her mind. While Caleb couldn't help feeling elated by the letter, he felt sympathetic too. Harriet Peabody-Penobscot had discarded her companion with as much care as she might throw out yesterday's newspaper.

He patted Justin's back. Thank goodness Miss Peabody hadn't made the trip to Texas. He cringed to think of anyone that cold-hearted caring for his boy. Caleb said a silent prayer of thanks.

Eleanor paced back and forth, rage burning in her eyes. "Why, that woman is nothing more than a…"

"Aunt Eleanor," Caleb said quietly. "We have children present."

She stopped her pacing and nodded. "Right. And we have a wedding to plan, don't we, Abigail?"

Abigail lifted her gaze and blinked several times. "I beg your pardon?"

Eleanor looked aghast, first at Caleb, then at Abigail and finally back to Caleb. "You *still* haven't proposed?"

"No, ma'am. But I intend to now."

Eleanor bit her lip. "Try to be charming. Would you like me to stay? I can be very persuasive and charming as well. Perhaps I should fetch my jewels. Abigail could pick out whatever suited her or have the entire lot if she doesn't want to decide. After all, a bride shouldn't have to pick just one thing."

"I think I can manage." Caleb smiled at Abigail who looked too stunned to give an answering smile.

"Besides," Caleb went on, "Justin will help me."

After Eleanor hurried out of the parlor with Dr. Whitacre in tow, Caleb went to Abigail. He set the baby in her arms and knelt before her. She blushed and gave him a shy smile.

"Miss Abigail, will you do me the honor of becoming my wife?"

Her eyes glistened with happy tears. "Yes, Mr. Walker. I would love nothing more."

Lifting his hand to her face, he cupped her jaw, leaned forward and brushed a soft kiss across her lips.

# Chapter Twenty-One

**Abigail**

The next morning, Eleanor came to her room accompanied by the cook who carried a breakfast tray. The woman set it down on a table in the corner of the bedroom. Eleanor waited until she was gone.

Abigail sat in a chair by the window, holding Justin as he finished his bottle.

"I took the liberty of sending for the pastor. I'd heard he intended to travel this week and was eager to have you two married."

Married! Abigail's mind was too busy and filled with disbelief to imagine such a thing. She felt as though she moved in a dream. A wonderful dream but a dream, nonetheless. Her gaze lingered on the baby. Her heart warmed as it always did when she looked at him.

"All right," she said softly, stroking the baby's cheek. "I still can hardly believe it."

"You belong to us, here in Texas." Eleanor closed the distance between them. Her eyes shone with deep emotion. "And we belong to you."

Abigail blinked back tears. Eleanor's words meant the world to her. All along, when she'd yearned for Caleb's smile or touch, she'd been wracked with guilt. He wasn't hers. She had to leave and couldn't hope for anything more than what she'd always had. In the space of a moment, maybe two, all that had washed away.

Eleanor took the baby so Abigail could dress. She carried him out of the room, leaving Abigail alone once more.

By the time Abigail went downstairs, she found Eleanor holding Justin, who was still dressed in a sleeping gown. It was fresh and clean, however. He wore a smile, evidently pleased to see the small crowd gathered in the parlor. Even Dr. Whitacre was there.

Caleb, dressed in a coat, tie, starched shirt, trousers and boots, looked handsome as ever. He made her heart race at the look in his eyes. His gaze was both tender and protective. A shimmer of awareness washed over her skin as he took her hands in his.

The marriage might be one of convenience. They hadn't even spoke of any details, but no matter what happened, she'd always have this moment and the way he gazed at her with longing.

The pastor was a younger man than the one who had given the sermon the prior Sunday. He'd been called in from a nearby town as a favor to their pastor.

He stood on the bottom step and beckoned them closer.

Caleb held her hands and faced her as they said their vows. When she said her part, Caleb slipped a band on her finger. She let out a soft breath as if the ring was the final proof of their union and up until that point, she'd scarcely believed it true.

"It's not very fancy," Eleanor whispered.

Abigail frowned. "Pardon me?"

"We'll get you something better. Caleb picked it out and it's very plain."

"Eleanor," Caleb said. "I'm standing two feet from you. I can hear you."

"It's fine." She gave Abigail a sheepish, apologetic look and patted Caleb's shoulder. "For now."

A few moments later, the pastor was on his way back to his own flock.

The family gathered to eat breakfast, a slightly more elaborate breakfast than usual. After, Caleb excused himself with the explanation of work he needed to do. Dr. Whitacre was the next to leave. Eleanor announced she hadn't slept a wink and needed a nap.

The day, from that point on, continued much like other days. Abigail would not allow herself to feel sorry for herself. The nuptials had been a hasty affair, to be sure. Probably because Caleb worried that she'd change her mind.

She tried not to think about what it might have been like to spend the day with her husband. The notion that they might be together their first day as man and wife tugged at her heart.

By supper, he was still gone. Eleanor had remained in bed with a headache. Abigail ate by herself with only Justin for company. After the meal, she gave the boy a bath and a bottle. She rocked him to sleep, holding him a little longer than usual and taking comfort as she held him in her arms.

When she began to nod off, she decided it was time to go to bed. The day had taxed her more than she realized. A bath beforehand sounded like a pleasant way to spend the rest of a lonely evening.

She laid the boy in his bed and tucked him in.

Standing by his crib, she watched him sleep. The lamplight flickered across his sweet face. Small sleep smiles tugged at his lips. He looked just like a tiny angel, sleeping beneath his blanket. His hair, soft as down, invited her fingertips. Unable to resist, she stroked his head as gently as she dared.

She could have stood by his crib for an age, admiring him as he slept. A deep contentment came over her. Ever since she'd arrived in Sweet Willow, she tried her best not to get too attached to the boy. She didn't want to let her heart love him so fiercely. Every day, she lost the battle a little more as her tender feelings for the boy grew.

And now she was here to stay. She could let herself love the boy, let herself grow attached. She could write down his milestones and look forward to all the things he would do in the months and years to come. The peace she felt, knowing she would be with him from this day on, was unlike anything else she'd ever known. It was powerful and all-encompassing.

With a soft prayer of thanksgiving, she bid the boy good night and left the nursery.

She went to her room and entered the washroom to find the tub occupied. Caleb lay in a steaming bath, regarding her with bemusement. Only his head, shoulders and arms were visible, but the shock of finding a man in her washroom astonished her. She let out a half-shriek.

He arched a mocking brow. "Terribly sorry, Miss Abigail."

She backed away a few steps, so she stood well outside the washroom. "You don't look at all sorry."

He moved, lifting in the water. She yelped and held out her hands as if that might prevent him from getting out. He remained in the tub, however, leaning over the edge and keeping his gaze fixed upon her with an unwavering, mischievous grin.

"The tub I use was moved to Eleanor's room." He shrugged. "I had no choice but to use the tub belonging to my *wife*."

Abigail shook her head with disbelief. "You, sir, are a rogue. Do not move. Do not move a single muscle." She tiptoed closer to the door and grasped the handle. "I shall close the door so you can bathe in private."

He opened his mouth to give her a reply, but she was too quick for him, shutting the door before he could get out a single teasing word. She hurried to the hallway to listen for Justin. She wasn't sure how well the sound of her distress might have traveled. Hopefully the noise hadn't woken the child, or Eleanor.

There was a sound. A soft bump. Or so she thought. She tiptoed down the hallway and stopped outside the nursery. No other sounds greeted her ear. It was quiet here in the nursery and throughout the house.

When she was sure the baby slept peacefully, she walked down the hallway to her room. She paused in the doorway and eyed the room warily. She'd assumed she would remain tonight and for the nights that would follow. Their marriage was a marriage of convenience, or so she thought.

She smiled, thinking about the look on Caleb's face when he'd startled her. He'd enjoyed startling her. She recalled how he'd kissed her that morning and last night as well when she accepted his offer of marriage. Lifting her hand slowly, she touched her lips and remembered the feel of his kiss.

She heard the door of the washroom as it opened. She crept into her room and found him in the doorway. He wore a pair of striped pajamas. His feet were bare. Water droplets dripped from his hair and down his face. His garments stuck to his body as if affixed by glue or a sticky substance.

"Did you dry off?" The moment she asked, she felt foolish. Clearly, he hadn't dried off. Behind him lay wet, puddled footprints. The tub drained with a chugging sound.

"I did not dry off."

"I see. Is that one of your customs, Mr. Walker? To sneak into a woman's washroom, use her tub and then dress in your nightclothes without using a towel?"

"No, Miss Abigail. I can attest to the fact that I have never done any of those things before."

"Why start now?"

"The reason I did not use a towel this evening is because I forgot to bring my towel. I did not see one in the washroom and did not want to alarm you further by asking you to bring me a towel – on account of how just a moment ago you screeched when you found me in the tub."

"You are as charming as the day is long."

"Thank you kindly."

"Would you like me to fetch you a towel from the linen closet?"

His lips quirked. "Don't you reckon it's too late?"

She went down the hallway to the linen cabinet. He followed two steps behind. She pulled a towel from the top shelf, patted his face and then his neck. He thanked her, took the towel from her and rubbed the back of his neck and hair.

The lamplight flickered, casting a soft warm glow over his face. His smile faded as he closed the distance between them. Her heartbeat raced as he drew near and took her hand in his.

He lifted her hand to his lips and kissed it. "I didn't put a proper ring on your finger this morning."

"Well... that's all right. We didn't have much time to prepare. Besides, I like a simple gold band."

"I want to get a ring for you. One that's never been on another woman's hand. Just yours."

His tone, as much as his words, brought a lump to her throat.

"All your clothes are from Harriet. Your shoes. Everything."

"I don't mind."

A growl rumbled in his chest. "I mind. I don't want my Abigail to have other people's castoffs. Not even Eleanor's."

She nodded. Her eyes stung.

"That's something we're doing soon. This week. Getting you dresses and shoes that were made for you. Picked out by you. Belong only to you. And a ring too."

"All right."

"I'm sorry I had to leave. I had to tend to a lame horse."

"I understand."

"I missed you," he said softly.

"I missed you too."

The quiet stretched between them. He held her hand and kept his gaze locked on hers. It seemed there was more he intended to say. Part of her wished he would go on and say what was on his heart. The other part of her prayed he wouldn't say another word.

The next sound, however, came not from him or any other person in the house. The sound, an eerie wail, came from the outside, a creature that prowled off in the darkness. The ghostly howl pierced the night. Almost at once, a chorus of yipping and baying followed.

"Oh," she breathed. "Coyotes."

A spark of amusement lit his eyes. "They're just tryin' to make a living, Miss Abigail."

"I wish they didn't make such a noisy fuss while they made their living, Mr. Walker."

He tilted his head toward his door, just a few paces from where they stood. "You could come to my room. I'd be sure to keep them away."

She held her breath, her mind whirring with a thousand reasons why she should refuse.

He tugged her closer into his embrace and lowered to press his lips to hers. He wrapped his arms around her a little more tightly. His arms felt strong and sheltering. She felt certain he could feel her thundering heartbeat. The glow of the candles lit his eyes with a tender warmth.

"Come with me, Abigail," he said gently. "And I promise to keep you safe. There's nothing I want more."

She nodded and let him lead her down the hall to his room.

# Chapter Twenty-Two

*Four months later*

**Caleb**

The family sat together, watching Justin manage his latest feat. Sitting up. The small boy lay on a blanket. He struggled and worked so hard to sit up that Caleb had the urge to help him with his task. Caleb sat in the parlor across from Eleanor and Abigail while Justin flailed around on the rug between them. The boy rolled from his stomach to his back and then to his stomach again. He fussed and grimaced.

Caleb resolved not to help the boy. It was best if Justin learned on his own. That would teach the boy independence. Caleb shifted uncomfortably on the edge of his chair. Justin caught sight of his movement and gave him what appeared very much like a pleading look. Caleb couldn't stand it. He rose from the chair, only to get a chiding look from Eleanor.

Caleb sighed and sank back to the chair.

"He can manage," Abigail said with a smile.

"Poor little fella. Pretty soon I'll have him out herding cattle with me. A day in the saddle's got to be more gratifying than learning to sit and stand and whatnot. How do any of us ever manage?"

Eleanor nodded. "If I can manage with a cane, he'll do just fine. You watch. Soon he'll be crawling, walking and then running. Your home will never be the same. Your *life* will never be the same."

The boy pushed himself up on his hands and knees. He rocked back and forth a time or two and then slumped over to a sitting position. His swayed precariously, his arms flailing but he gained control and steadied himself. With a broad grin, he looked around the room as if to see if his audience had noticed his success. He clapped and laughed in delight. His smile revealed two teeth on his lower jaw.

Caleb thought the boy's smile was one of the finest things he knew. And his laughter always made Caleb laugh along with anyone else in hearing distance. Eleanor watched the boy, her eyes glistening.

Caleb remained in the parlor with Abigail and Eleanor for as long as he could, finally excusing himself to go to work. His men were probably waiting. If they knew he was sitting in the parlor watching a baby practice sitting up, he'd never hear the end of it.

Abigail followed him out, leaving Eleanor with the baby.

She stopped on the porch to receive his kiss. He lingered, savoring a few more of her kisses. Wrapping his arms around her, he drew a deep breath.

"You fit perfectly in my arms, Miss Abigail."

"It's my favorite spot, Mr. Walker. I especially like to rest my head against your shoulder while I fall asleep."

"I'm mighty fond of having you there too. I can't imagine you anywhere else."

A buggy came over the hill. It was too far off to see who was coming.

"That's Laura and Francine," Abigail said. "Laura's going to measure Justin for a new jumper." She looked up at him, her eyes growing somber. "I believe I'll need some newborn gowns as well."

Caleb stared, not comprehending at first, and then smiled broadly. He lowered to kiss her tenderly. "That's wonderful news, sweetheart."

Setting his palm on her waist, he tried to imagine their little one. Contentment warmed his heart. His heart was so full already. It was impossible to imagine greater joy. When he'd proposed to Abigail, he yearned for a life with her by his side. He hadn't dared to hope that one day the two of them would be man and wife and have children of their own.

Abigail set her hand on his and held it to her stomach. She gave a breathless laugh. "I'm so happy."

"I am too. I can hardly believe the news."

"I think we can expect this little one sometime near Christmas."

He heard her words catch in her throat. He cupped her jaw and stroked his thumb across her cheek. "Something troubling you?"

"I'm grateful. I feel blessed. Every day I thank God for the wonderful things he's given me. I never, ever imagined a life like this. I never dared to hope for so much happiness. I love my family so much that my heart feels as though it might overflow." She glanced over her shoulder at the approaching buggy.

"What is it?"

"I don't know if I should tell Laura. She's prayed for a baby ever since she arrived in Texas. She wants to give Seth a son more than anything in the world."

Caleb knew Seth Bailey wanted children and couldn't fault him for wanting a son. Still, he couldn't understand preferring a son over a daughter. Perhaps it was because he already had a son. Just the same, a child, either son or daughter, was a blessing.

"You'd best tell Laura," he said quietly. "She's been a good friend to you. I'm certain she'll be happy for you. What's more, I don't believe she'll take kindly to you keeping the news to yourself."

"That's what Eleanor said."

"Eleanor?" Caleb grumbled, trying to suppress a smile. "You mean to tell me that my aunt got the good news before I did? Something's wrong with that order of events, Miss Abigail."

"I didn't tell her first, Mr. Walker. She guessed over a week ago. One morning over breakfast she flat-out told me that I was in the family way."

Caleb groaned, feigning deep dismay. "Land sakes. Now we're in trouble. She's likely started a list of names for the baby. She'll test each and every one by writing it out next to *Admiral*. I'm sure she's already planned the child's military career."

"Your aunt thinks it's going to be a girl. You can guess what name she suggested."

"I bet I know." He chuckled as he descended the steps and waited for Laura to arrive. When she pulled the buggy to a stop, he lifted her down and did the same for Francine.

"Good morning to you, ladies," he said. Francine and Laura offered a polite hello. He took the horse and buggy to the barn so his men could tend to things. As he reached the barn, he looked back to the house to glimpse Laura and Abigail embracing.

Throughout the day, he thought of Abigail and the wonder of the baby she expected. His joy gave way to worry. His worry faded when the joy returned.

He intended to remain near the barn in case Abigail might need something but had to leave in the late afternoon. A cow had gotten trapped in the muddy banks of a pond. He and several men rode out to help free the struggling creature.

By the time he returned, it was long past dark. The house was quiet. Justin slumbered in his crib. Abigail, already dressed in her sleeping gown, had fallen asleep on the chesterfield in the sitting room. He smiled, crossed the room to pick her up, but paused to admire her as she dozed in the lamplight.

His heart swelled with tenderness. He loved her more than he could say. In fact, he hadn't said anything of his love for her. He'd need to remedy that immediately.

Lifting her in his arms, he caught a scent of her honeyed skin and bent to kiss her forehead. He carried her easily up the stairs and to their room. She sighed as he set her gently on the bed.

"Caleb," she murmured. "I missed you."

"I missed you. I always miss you when I'm away." He thought of his intention to tell her about his deep and abiding affection. Why did the words always feel so clumsy, so unbearably awkward? Tonight wasn't the night. He'd wait for the perfect moment. "Did you have a nice visit with Laura?"

Her lids fluttered and drifted up. She gazed at him. Her eyes lit with sadness. "It was lovely. It's always nice to see her and Francine."

"Frankie?"

Abigail's lips twitched. "She's only Frankie when she's out riding with Noah and Seth. Today she was back to Francine. I must say I like that name better."

"Maybe insisting on being called Frankie is just a stage."

"Maybe so."

Caleb went to the washroom and found a basin of tepid water. He stripped off his dusty work clothes, washed and donned his pajamas. Returning to the bedroom, he fixed his gaze on her as he buttoned his shirt. "How was Laura?"

Abigail pursed her lips and drew a heavy sigh. "She made a show of being happy for me, but I could tell she's grown desperate to start on her own family. As much as she loves Francine, she still wants a baby to hold. And she wants to give Seth a boy to carry on the Bailey name."

He blew out the lamp, got into bed and drew Abigail into his arms. "It will happen. All in God's perfect timing."

She rested against his shoulder. Almost instantly, her breathing deepened. She sank against him as sleep came for her. The speed with which she fell asleep gave him new fodder for his worrying mind. Had she done too much? Justin likely wore her out. Perhaps he should find a helper for her. He lay in the darkness, his mind turning over a score of worries.

# Chapter Twenty-Three

**Abigail**

The next morning, she awoke alone in their bed. Her first thought concerned Justin, as usual, and she listened intently for a sign that he was awake. The house was quiet, however, not even a sound from Caleb. He'd probably left already.

The sky was overcast, darkening the house. A rumble of thunder rolled across the distant hills.

She knelt, said her prayers, washed and dressed. By the time she had her hair done, she heard the faint stirrings from the nursery. Hurrying into Justin's room, she found him with his small hands wrapped around the edge of the crib, trying to pull himself up.

"Look at my clever boy," she crooned.

Lifting him out of the crib, she drew in the scent of the special soap Eleanor bought for him. It was a pleasant, citrus scent, a smell that met with the approval of his father. Caleb had found the first few soaps that Eleanor brought for him to be too floral. Too fussy.

"I don't want my son to smell like a bunch of daisies," he'd grumbled one morning at breakfast.

"Daisies don't smell like flowers," Dr. Whitacre said before Eleanor could argue. "They smell like cow manure."

Caleb and Dr. Whitacre shared a hearty laugh.

Eleanor had been irritated with both men and proceeded to try different varieties that met with masculine approval. She went on to explain that she hoped the new soaps didn't smell like flowers or manure.

Dr. Whitacre still came once a week. Abigail suspected it was to see Eleanor. When he arrived, he sought her out immediately, barely giving the baby a passing glance. And Eleanor seemed pleased to have him visit. Lately, she scarcely returned to her home in Houston.

Abigail spent the morning tending to the baby. Feeding him. Reading a story book to him and taking him for a walk on the porch. The clouds grew darker and the thunder that had sounded far off grew louder. Lightning forked the sky, striking the fields off in the distance.

The clouds churned. The warm winds blew, sweeping across the ranch, blowing leaves and branches. A limb fell from the pecan tree on the side of the house. Abigail hurried inside with Justin in her arms. They watched from the window as the storm gathered.

She wished fervently that Caleb were home. She moved from room to room, searching the surroundings for her husband. The sound of Eleanor's cane thudded on the steps.

"We need to get into the cellar," she said without preliminaries. "Right away."

"Yes, all right."

They hurried to the door under the stairwell. Eleanor ushered her in first and followed a step behind. The cellar, mostly below ground, had windows that allowed for some light. Abigail had never been downstairs. Her heart raced frantically.

When she reached the bottom of the steps, she looked at Eleanor expectantly.

Eleanor shrugged a slender shoulder. "Now we wait."

Abigail tightened her hold on Justin. Eleanor sighed as she looked around the cellar. "When Caleb redid the house, I told him he didn't need a storm cellar, but I suppose the boy knew what he was doing."

The door opened. Caleb raced down the steps and gathered Abigail into his arms. "Are you alright?"

"I'm fine," Abigail replied.

"I am too," Eleanor remarked drily. "Aside from missing part of my nap."

A drumming noise reverberated through the house. As it grew louder and faster, even Eleanor's expression changed from bored indifference to dismay. Her eyes widened as she grew more fearful.

"I recall a twister coming through my uncle's town when I was a child," she said. "The winds tossed houses and carriages around like they were mere toys."

The wind howled and shook the house.

Caleb took his aunt by the hand and led her to a chair. She walked unsteadily and fell into the chair heavily. Her face was ashen. She trembled.

Abigail didn't know Eleanor had it in her to be afraid of anything. The woman faced every challenge squarely. This was different and for some reason, Eleanor's fear made Abigail determined not to give in to her own fear. Instead, she said a silent prayer, asking for strength. The winds gusted even more ferociously, but her heart calmed.

"It's going to be all right, Aunt Eleanor," Caleb said quietly.

He took off his coat and laid it over her shoulders. She clasped his hand and gave it a squeeze. "My sweet boy."

Caleb returned to Abigail and Justin. By now, the boy whimpered. He arched in Abigail's arms, seeking out his father's arms. Caleb took him, held him snugly and spoke soothingly to him. He wrapped his other arm around Abigail.

The sounds grew to a deafening roar. Abigail clung to Caleb. She wrapped her arms around both her husband and son. Caleb spoke. At first, she couldn't understand him but then as the sounds faded, she could tell that he prayed. When he finished, he kissed her head.

"I love you, Abigail. You were the blessing I prayed for." She looked up at him to find his gaze upon her, his eyes filled with a soft expression. The noise of the drumming diminished and slowed. He kept his eyes on her. "With all my heart, I love you."

The wind blew, whistling an eerie cry.

Caleb went on. "I meant to tell you last night – all the ways I love you, but I didn't. I love the way you purse your lips when you read. I love the way your eyes light up when you smile."

The last of the banging faded, leaving only the lonesome sound of the wind.

He continued. "And I love the way you love Justin and the way you love me."

"I love you too," she replied softly.

Lowering, he pressed a kiss to her lips.

The storm faded from her awareness. All she could think of was the comfort of having Caleb close and holding Justin in her arms. She stood in the circle of his arms. The storm might have destroyed the world but as long as she had Caleb and Justin nothing else mattered.

She rested her head against his chest and closed her eyes.

Eleanor grumbled and banged her cane, startling Abigail.

"Do you mean to tell me this is the first time you've told your wife those three words?" The woman's imperious tone had returned as the winds blew the storm further from the ranch.

"I'm afraid so," Caleb replied.

Abigail felt her lips tug into a smile. "It's all right, Aunt Eleanor. It was worth the wait."

"I should say not. I knew that wooing and courting wouldn't be his strong suit."

"He has so many other qualities," Abigail defended, her smile widening.

Caleb helped his aunt out of the chair. "Have I told you I loved you today, Aunt Eleanor?"

"You have not."

"Well, I love you too."

"You'd better!" she exclaimed.

"Can you make it up the stairs on your own?"

Eleanor knit her brows. "You hush." She swatted his shoulder. "Don't you sass me."

Once upstairs, they found the storm had come and gone, leaving only broken tree limbs in its wake. Rain fell for a short while. By nightfall, the skies cleared, and a quiet peace descended once again.

# Chapter Twenty-Four

*Thanksgiving*

**Caleb**

The baby wasn't supposed to come until Christmas. That's what Abigail guessed. Caleb couldn't say for certain. They'd been married ten months and lived together as man and wife since the wedding. His sweet wife certainly looked ready to have her little one, but no one had asked him.

He paced back and forth, frowning. No, it didn't make a lick of sense. It wasn't up to him when the baby arrived. Just the same, he wasn't ready. If he'd had a choice in the matter, he would have held off a few more weeks.

Raking his fingers through his hair, he grimaced.

"You're going to wear yourself out." Eleanor sat on the chesterfield.

Not once in his life had he seen his aunt with yarn in her hands. She wasn't one for handiwork. And yet, there she was, sitting as prim and proper as a lady in Queen Victoria's court, knitting. *Knitting.*

Beside her sat a basket with the fruits of her labor, a half dozen booties, bright yellow booties. She'd insisted the baby was a girl but hedged her bets with yellow yarn.

Beside her, Justin slept in his cradle. The boy was almost too big for the cradle. He was a sturdy boy, strong and growing fast. Caleb watched the child doze and felt his shoulders loosen. Something about watching the boy sleep always gave him a sense of peace. He lowered to brush a kiss over the boy's head.

Eleanor shooed him away and he went back to pacing the far side of the room.

A noise came from upstairs. Caleb hurried to the foot of the staircase and listened intently, hardly daring to breathe. The only sound he could hear was the voice of Dr. Whitacre talking to the nurse he'd brought along to help.

"They won't forget to announce the girl's arrival," Eleanor said from the parlor.

Caleb returned. "Seems like I should be up there."

"They'll be fine, Caleb. Babies are born every day."

He supposed that was true. In a way. He considered the notion a little more. Yes. Babies *were* born every day. The idea settled in his mind. He chuckled. For some reason, ever since Abigail's labor had started that morning, the fact that women had been giving birth for a long time hadn't entered into his thinking.

"What do you think of the name Sarah?" Eleanor wrinkled her nose and fixed her gaze upon him. "Abigail says she always dreamed she had a sister named Sarah."

"She's told me that. I think Sarah is a nice name. Sounds like it means a lot to Abigail."

This was a thorny subject. While Abigail and Eleanor loved each other deeply, there had been a few differences of opinion on the baby's name. Eleanor's tone suggested, strongly, that it would behoove him to dismiss the name Sarah and go with another name. Possibly the name Eleanor.

His wife, however, lay upstairs laboring to bring their child into the world. Out of loyalty, he should side with his wife.

He weighed his options. "I suppose the mama should have her say."

Eleanor sniffed and returned her attention to the yellow bootie.

A slight pang of guilt touched his heart. It wasn't Eleanor's place to suggest the child be named after her, but she'd never been able to have children of her own, and shouldn't her feelings count? That had been the argument she'd presented each evening at the dinner table for the last week.

Abigail had only offered a mysterious smile. She refused to make a decision until the child arrived. Caleb wanted to point out that the baby might be a boy. He'd gotten the distinct feeling that neither his wife nor his aunt bothered discussing a boy's name.

"There was a girl at finishing school named Sarah," Eleanor said. "I didn't care for her bossy, know-it-all ways."

"So you knew a girl named Sarah. You never mentioned anything about that. The truth comes out."

He could see she was about to correct him for his cheeky ways. The sound of a door opening stopped her from saying a word. She set her knitting aside. Caleb sprang to his feet and rushed to the stairs.

The nurse came down the stairs, a smile lighting her face. "You can come up now, Mr. Walker."

Forgetting entirely about Eleanor, Caleb ran up the stairs, taking them two at a time. He dashed to the bedroom but slowed as he came to the door. He didn't want to startle Abigail by rushing into the room.

Dr. Whitacre greeted him, looking tired but pleased. His eyes held a hint of disbelief. "Haven't had this happen since medical school."

A jolt of terror hit Caleb like a punch to the chest. Without bothering to ask, he pushed past the doctor. Abigail lay in bed. She held the child in her arms and offered him an exhausted smile.

Slowly, he moved to the bed. He fell to his knees. She tugged the blanket back to show off her new baby.

"Meet your son, Mr. Walker."

"A boy," he whispered.

The baby regarded him with a thoughtful expression. Caleb hadn't realized newborns could do anything other than cry. Justin had certainly howled when he was a newborn, the poor little thing.

"He's beautiful," Caleb said. He gave her a tender look. "You're beautiful. Our family is growing."

Abigail shifted in the bed to reveal another small bundle beside her. Caleb leaned in for a closer look. The bundle moved, emitting a small cry.

Caleb blinked several times, wondering if his eyes played tricks on him.

"Twin boys," Abigail said.

The blood drained from his face. Of all the frightening scenarios that had played out in his thoughts, he hadn't considered the possibility of Abigail having twins.

"Both boys are perfectly healthy, Caleb." Dr. Whitacre spoke. "They're both as strong as any child I've delivered. You need not worry just because they're twins."

Eleanor came to the door, leaning heavily on her cane. She gave a mischievous grin. "Where's baby Eleanor?"

Dr. Whitacre went to her side and kissed her on the cheek. "Twins, Ellie. A couple of boys. Two healthy, handsome and robust Walker boys."

It took a moment for Eleanor to recover her senses. Slowly, with an expression of disbelief, she moved to the side of Abigail's bed. She remained very still and gazed in stunned disbelief. After a long moment, finally comprehending what she saw – that there were two babies, not one, she set her hand over her heart and let out a teary sigh.

After a moment more, she recovered her senses and bent to kiss Abigail's forehead. With a bemused smile, she eyed Caleb. She patted her hair, with the unspoken reminder that it had turned gray so many years ago on account of Caleb and his brother. "You, my dear boy, are going to have your hands full."

"Just the way I like things in my home," Caleb replied. He took Abigail's hand as his heart filled with warmth and love. "It's what I yearned for all along."

# Chapter Twenty-Five

*Boston*

**Sarah**

She lifted the heavy brass knocker and let it fall, listening to the resounding boom as she summoned her courage. Bravery. Valor. That was what she needed. Money would help too, since most of her meager inheritance had been spent on her trip to Boston.

Footsteps echoed in the hallway inside the grand home. A maid opened the door. The young woman knit her brow and let her gaze drift from Sarah's face down to her boots and back up again.

From the maid's expression, Sarah guessed she passed her scrutiny. The rose damask gown had been the right choice. Thank goodness. Sarah had fretted about the right thing to wear to such a fancy home.

"May I help you?"

"I hope so." Sarah's voice faltered. She cleared her throat and stole a quick glance at the tattered letter. "I'm looking for my sister, Abigail Winthrop."

The maid blinked and shook her head. "I'm sorry. This is the Penobscot residence. Reginald and Harriet Penobscot."

The sound of a baby's cry drifted from the home. Footsteps echoed up the stairs. A woman's voice murmured comforting words. A moment later, the crying stopped.

The maid smiled. "And the home of young Reggie. Mustn't forget the new baby."

"My sister grew up at the Mill Street Home."

The maid grimaced. "I'm sorry to hear that, but I'm not sure what it has to do with the Penobscot family."

"I was told that Mrs. Penobscot's parents took my sister in when she was ten or so."

"Who is it, Gemma?" came a woman's voice from inside.

"A lady looking for an Abigail Winthrop. I told her there's no one here by that name."

The maid's words were greeted with silence. Sarah held her breath. If the Penobscot family couldn't tell her where she might find Abigail, she might never find her sister. A weight fell upon her shoulders. Her throat tightened. She hadn't known she had a sister until a month ago. She'd come all the way to Boston to meet her.

"Show her into the parlor," the woman said.

The maid beckoned Sarah inside and led her through the foyer to an elegant sitting room. The room was filled with an array of fine furnishings. Near the windows sat a table with a vase of lilacs. A piano took up part of the corner.

A fire, burning cheerfully in the hearth, brightened the room and gladdened Sarah's heart. After the walk to the Penobscot home, she felt a chill all the way to her bones.

"Miss Sarah Winthrop, to see you, Mrs. Penobscot," the maid said. She curtsied and left the room.

Mrs. Penobscot sat on a chesterfield, a baby in her arms, cooing to the child. She gestured to a chair on the other side.

Sarah sank to the chair, grateful for the fire's warmth. The woman fussed over the baby for a few moments while Sarah waited.

A nursemaid entered the room, a bottle in hand.

"Time for lunch, my little princeling," Mrs. Penobscot murmured. She gave the boy a kiss on the head and let the nursemaid take him from her arms.

Sarah resisted the urge to blurt out a thousand questions about Abigail. She'd waited a lifetime. She could wait a little longer. Another servant entered the room, carrying a silver platter heaped with cakes, cookies and bonbons. After she left, Mrs. Penobscot eyed her while nibbling a gingersnap.

"You're her sister." She finished her cookie, took a sip of tea and studied the assortment of sweets. She selected another treat and ate it thoughtfully. "I didn't know Abigail had a sister."

Sarah almost fainted from relief. Mrs. Penobscot's words confirmed what she had scarcely dared to hope. Abigail was her sister. It had taken over a month to get to Boston. With every mile that Sarah traveled from California, she'd tried to talk herself out of any false hope of a sister. A shimmer of excitement washed over her at the thought she might finally come face to face with Abigail. Perhaps that very day.

"I didn't know I had a sister either," Sarah said. "The news came as a lovely surprise."

The woman nodded. "You're as pretty as Abigail."

Sarah's face warmed. Ever since she found her parents' letters, she'd wondered if she might resemble her long-lost sister. The possibility filled her with a heady rush of happiness.

"I should mention my surname is not Winthrop."

Mrs. Penobscot blinked. "Go on."

"My last name is Becker. My parents passed away. I was adopted by an elderly German couple, Otto and Erna Becker."

Sarah pursed her lips to keep from saying too much more. If she started talking about the Beckers, she might talk half the morning. The Beckers had been kind not only to her but to everyone they met. They'd taught Sarah everything they knew, and together the family ran a busy little shop in San Francisco. Now was not the time to talk about all her happy memories.

She leaned forward, her heart thudding. "Do you know where I can find my sister?"

Mrs. Penobscot heaved a deep sigh. Sarah found her gaze drawn to the woman's dress bodice, wondering if the seams might give way under the strain.

Another maid entered the room carrying a fresh pot of tea. She set it down on the table and turned to leave when Mrs. Penobscot stopped her.

"I don't like these little powdery round balls. What are they?"

The maid peered at the tray. "I'm not sure, Mrs. Penobscot."

"They must have a name. Who went to the candy store today?"

The girl reddened. "I did."

Mrs. Penobscot's brow creased. "Well? What did the shopkeeper call them?"

The girl's mouth opened and snapped close.

"Truffles," Sarah said. "They're called chocolate truffles. The powder is cocoa. You can buy them with cocoa, without cocoa or with dark chocolate sprinkles or milk chocolate sprinkles. Sometimes they make them with shaved dark chocolate, but I don't recommend that variety." She listed the options, stopping herself just shy of giving prices for the sweets because that would have been absurd, of course.

She wasn't standing behind the shop counter, wearing her striped apron.

Mrs. Penobscot's jaw dropped a fraction. Her expression of mild boredom was replaced with growing interest. Sarah felt a flush of self-consciousness. She hadn't intended to be a chatterbox. Her memories stirred. She could almost hear Erna Becker chuckling and Otto grumbling about chatting with every customer that came to their shop.

The maid muttered a few words of apology and hurried away.

"You know about sweets?" Mrs. Penobscot's mouth curved into a smile. "Perhaps I should offer you a cup of tea."

Sarah demurred. "No thank you, I'm eager to find my sister."

"Are you a baker?"

"No. I'm a candy maker."

Mrs. Penobscot's eyes flashed. She let out an inelegant yelp followed by a breathless laugh. "Really? Perhaps I should offer you a cup of tea *and* employment."

"Thank you kindly, but I won't rest until-"

"I know. I know. Until you find your sister. Well, she's not here. She sailed to Texas. I'm not sure if she remained."

"Texas?" Sarah's heart sank. "Do you happen to know where in Texas?"

Mrs. Penobscot got an odd sort of look on her face. "No, I'm afraid I don't recall where she ended up. She was to accompany me to Texas when I briefly considered marrying a gentleman there." She lowered her voice to a whisper. "It might come as a bit of a shock, but there was a time I'd considered becoming a mail-order bride."

"My goodness."

"And now," she went on, no longer speaking in a whisper, "I'm married to a man who made his fortune in fishing. They call my husband the King of Cod."

Sarah bit her lip to keep from smiling at the name. It wouldn't do to giggle, not since she needed as much information as possible.

Mrs. Penobscot continued. "You might ask the Massachusetts Matchmakers. They made all the arrangements. I believe the gentleman I corresponded with went by the name of Williamson. No, it was Williams."

"Williams?"

"Or was it Watson?" Mrs. Penobscot tapped her chin. "The town was Sweet Willow. That's all I know."

Sarah's shoulders sank. She wanted to ask more but could see that Mrs. Penobscot didn't wish to discuss the subject further. It was clear she had confused all the names and couldn't be counted on.

*Williams, Watson, Sweet Willow.*

Mrs. Penobscot frowned and ate another cookie.

"I'll take my leave now," Sarah said, rising to her feet. "Thank you."

"The agency might not have a record of her whereabouts. But it's worth a try. Give them my name, as she was to sail with me to Texas. I'm afraid I didn't remain aboard. When the time came to leave, Abigail went without me."

There was something in Mrs. Penobscot's voice that hinted of remorse. Mrs. Penobscot might have intended to sail to Texas and marry, but Sarah could plainly see the woman had a change of heart. Where did that leave Abigail? She wouldn't rest until she had her answer.

Sarah nodded. "I intend to ask them. I've come all this way. Nothing will stop me from finding my sister."

*The End*

Book Two of Sweet Willow Mail Order Brides
Mail Order Sarah

Sarah Becker suspects her long-lost sister has traveled to Texas and married a rancher. Sarah yearns to find Abigail, the sister she's never known. She agrees to become a mail-order bride to a man in Texas. Noah, her husband to-be, is a gruff cowboy who never intended to marry. He needs a wife to help raise six orphaned boys.

*Books by Charlotte Dearing*

<u>Sweet Willow Mail Order Brides</u>
Mail Order Abigail
Mail Order Sarah
Mail Order Susanna

<u>Copper Creek Mail Order Brides</u>
Mail Order Ruth
Mail Order Rebecca
Mail Order Holly

<u>The Bluebonnet Brides Collection</u>
Mail Order Grace
Mail Order Rescue
Mail Order Faith
Mail Order Hope
Mail Order Destiny

<u>Brides of Bethany Springs Series</u>
To Charm a Scarred Cowboy
Kiss of the Texas Maverick
Vow of the Texas Cowboy
The Accidental Mail Order Bride
Starry-Eyed Mail Order Bride
An Inconvenient Mail Order Bride
Amelia's Storm

*and many others...*

Sign up at <u>www.charlottedearing.com</u> to be notified of special offers and announcements.

Printed in Great Britain
by Amazon